The Ghosts of Grang

by Geoffrey Sleight

Remember that it is not enough to abstain from lying by word of mouth; for the worst lies are often conveyed by a false look, smile, or act. **Abraham Cahan**

CHAPTER 1

EDDIE settled himself on a park bench. Life wasn't treating him well. His own fault he knew, but it was hard coming to terms with the fact. The blame for his downfall laid entirely on him.

He wondered about his next move, unaware that fate was already mapping a perilous future for him.

A middle-aged man, with side parted greying hair, and wearing a smart dark suit, approached and sat on the park bench a couple of spaces from him. Both men stared ahead, their eyes following ducks gliding on the park pond, quacking and occasionally dipping their heads for a nibble at food beneath the surface.

Strolling on the path in front of the bench, office workers took lunchtime fresh air breaks, mothers accompanied their chattering children.

Eddie's gaze changed to the spread of trees on an expansive lawn at the far side of the pond, thoughts still immersed in his woes. He'd had everything. His wonderful partner, Steph, the business they ran together, and a comfortable flat. Now he'd blown it all.

They'd met at a friend's party. She worked in a baker's shop, and as well as the standard fare of bread and rolls, Steph's wizardry at making delicious cakes became a successful addition to the range.

He worked at a restaurant, starting as a waiter, but progressing to preparing meals by learning skills from an acclaimed chef.

Eddie and Steph decided to leave these jobs, borrow money from the bank and open a restaurant in their Bedfordshire home town of Tollbridge, combining their skills to make meals, exquisite desserts and cakes.

"Lovely day, isn't it," the grey haired man broke into Eddie's memories. He turned and nodded. The bright August sunshine and gentle breeze combined to create a pleasantly comfortable temperature. The stranger smiled, the lines of middle age creasing his face, his eyes searching for communication. Eddie resumed staring across the pond, immersed in his thoughts again.

The couple's new business went well in the beginning. Novelty interest from the townsfolk. Praised by many. But after a few months, customer numbers began to decline. Eddie and Steph couldn't compete with the big chain restaurants on price and special offers.

"Taking a lunch break? the stranger interrupted Eddie's memory again. It annoyed him, but he returned another nod, and summoned a brief smile. Eddie could hardly afford a packet of crisps, let alone lunch. Now he reflected on his current financial status.

The takings for the restaurant began to decline. Eddie had taken charge of the accounts, and assured Steph all was well, even though the deficit began to mount. Secretly he took to online gambling in an attempt to reverse their fortune. It was a hopeless strategy as losses now began to increase on two fronts.

Then Steph opened a letter in the post Eddie hadn't been able to retrieve before her. It was a notification from the bank, that since the loan repayment on the restaurant had not been paid for six months, action was being taken to issue a repossession order.

"Why the hell didn't you let me know?" she screamed at him in their flat above the restaurant. "I trusted you!"

"I was trying to protect you from worrying about it" Eddie pleaded his excuse.

"I saw you doing online gambling sometimes, but I thought you were trying small punts for fun," Steph's anger continued to grow. "You were gambling to try and get repayment money, weren't you?"

Eddie couldn't deny it, and his attempts to calm her were forcefully rejected.

"You bloody fool, driving us towards bankruptcy. I can never trust you again," she shouted. "That's it. We're over!"

Salvation lay in the fact Steph's grandmother had gifted money in her will, which would be enough for Steph to pay off the repayment debt, and put the restaurant up for sale. But she had no intention of helping Eddie any further, even when he told her that his own bank account had been cancelled some weeks before, and without funding from the business account, he'd be virtually penniless.

"I don't bloody care. You made your bed, now go and lay in it," she'd told him, "you're not dragging me down any more. I'm going to stay at my parents for a while, until I can get the mess sorted. I'll be back here later to collect my things, and I hope not to see you here." Collecting her coat and handbag, she'd left.

Eddie continued to gaze at the pond. His depression stunned him into a stupor. How could he have been so recklessly stupid?

"You look rather troubled," the well spoken stranger interrupted his melancholy again. Eddie's inclination was to tell the man to mind his own business. He had enough to worry about, without some nosy parker intruding into his life. But with his emotions being occupied elsewhere at present, he couldn't be bothered to tell the man where to go.

In fact, the reverse happened. Eddie suddenly felt the need to pour out his heart to someone. A confessional therapy. Someone unknown who would likely have no judgemental attitude towards him.

"If you bloody well want to know, I'll tell you why," Eddie declared.

"Please do," the man replied calmly.

When he'd finished the tale of woe, the stranger gazed sympathetically at Eddie.

"We all take a wrong turn sometimes," his confessor observed, hoping to lessen the sense of guilt for him. "Just needs time to repair."

Eddie found himself beginning to warm to this newcomer in his life. Someone who didn't consider him worthless. Both men looked at the pond again as a flotilla of ducklings glided behind their mother across the water.

"I may be able to help you," the stranger spoke, breaking the brief silence. Eddie was unsure how to react. Help was certainly what he needed, but why would someone completely unknown to him want to assist. The man's expensive looking suit didn't mark him as a roaming charity worker searching for down and outs.

"Why would you want to help?" Eddie posed.

"I've had difficulties in my life," the stranger replied, "and knowing what it feels like, I empathise with you."

"You sound like an educated man," said Eddie, "like you live well off."

"I am and I do," the man admitted, "but that doesn't shield you from difficulties." His eyes appeared to reflect on memories of obstacles in his own life.

They gazed at the pond again. The duck brigade had taken a sweep across the water and now swung round to retrace their journey. A boy on a bike pulled up on the path in front of them, and leaned over to check the chain. Satisfied it was okay, he rode off.

"If you don't mind me saying, you look as though you've been dragged through a hedge then rolled in the dirt," the stranger said, studying Eddie's clothing.

"You're right," Eddie agreed, taking no offence. After separating from Steph, he had little money on him.

The small amount of cash he'd had in the flat was all that remained. It had been enough to afford two nights in a local bed and breakfast down the road from his former restaurant. But last night he bedded down behind a hedgerow in the park, not far from where he now sat. His only possessions were some clothes and toiletries in the travel bag resting beside the bench.

Eddie had been orphaned at eight years of age after his drug addict parents could no longer cope, and relatives didn't want to get involved. Growing up in an orphanage had put the wider family even further out of reach, so in that direction he had nowhere to turn for help or refuge.

He didn't want to burden a few of his closer friends, who were now living in other parts of the country, and he felt that his pride had been damaged enough without resorting to begging from them.

"I'm fairly wealthy," the stranger interrupted Eddie's drift into memory again. "You can stay at my country house for a while if it helps," he offered.

Any lifeline was welcome, but Eddie felt cautious of a generous offer from someone he didn't know.

"Who are you?" he probed.

"I'm a surgeon, and work at the specialist hospital here in Tollbridge. My name's Ernest Albright," he revealed.

Eddie was surprised to learn of the man's high status, particularly the fact he should be interested in such lowly company.

"I need a gardener and general maintenance man for the grounds of my country estate, and I'll pay a reasonable wage for the work," the consultant continued. "You'll also have your own room and free meals."

The work wasn't anything Eddie had considered pursuing in his life, but the prospect of not living rough was appealing. Trying to find work had been the next on his agenda, and now a job was falling into his lap.

His only worry lay in wondering if there was some ulterior motive for the lifeline offer. But even if there was, the surgeon would hardly be likely to tell him if asked. And right now, he was glad of being offered the refuge.

"That's really good of you," he said, accepting the offer. "I'm Eddie Cartwright."

"My pleasure," the consultant smiled, stretching out his hand to shake Eddie's. "I have a flat in town here," he continued, "where I'm largely based during the week near the hospital. My main home is near Coulton Regis in Sussex. The residence is called Harcourt Grange. Been in my family for generations."

Eddie was impressed. Ernest Albright came across as a man of great knowledge and wealth.

"Thing is," Eddie paused, feeling embarrassed, "I don't have enough money right now to get to your place in Sussex. I can hardly afford a bus ride across town."

The surgeon reached for his inside jacket pocket and produced a black leather wallet. Opening it, he counted out a generous amount of notes, more than enough for the train journey involved.

"That's for your travel from the station here, as well as a good meal, new shirt, shoes and trousers. I don't want you turning up looking like a tramp." He handed the money over.

Eddie's first thought on receiving it was that he could just walk away and spend it how he liked. Gamble it even. But that had only brought about his downfall, and the offer he'd received seemed to be a much better prospect for the time being. The surgeon gazed at him with invasive eyes, as if reading his thoughts.

"Thanks," said Eddie, giving a smile to indicate he could be trusted. "I'll catch the train today."

"There's one that leaves at 3.10 this afternoon," said the surgeon. "You'll have to make a change at Albany Station, and that'll take you directly to Coulton Regis," he said, standing up.

"I'll telephone ahead and tell my wife Edith to expect you. Our driver will collect you from the station," he added, and left.

Eddie remained on the bench a little longer, still wondering if there was some catch involved with this lucky break. It was an incredibly generous offer from a complete stranger. Better a bird in the hand though he decided, then went on his way.

CHAPTER 2

THE train passed through rich green pastures with views of woodlands, farmsteads and distant hills as it grew nearer to the destination.

Eddie was dressed in newly purchased blue shirt, navy chinos, a black bomber jacket and burgundy trainers. He sat enjoying the countryside scenery, relaxing for the first time in days. There were few other passengers in the carriage, and only one stepped off with him on arrival at Coulton Regis.

The station also had an air of relaxation too, with colourful flower borders decorating the rears of the platforms. At the exit gate the stationmaster waited with a smile.

"Welcome to Coulton Regis," came his cheery greeting. This rural setting was a far cry from the hurrying bustle of town life that Eddie knew so well. The man appeared to be in his sixties, but a life in fresh air softened the lines of his face.

"You look like a newcomer here," he continued. "Would you like me to call a cab for you? There's not much of a bus service."

"I'm staying at Harcourt Grange," Eddie replied. The smile on the man's face fell a little.

"Oh, right," the cheery tone faded too. "The driver's outside waiting for you. Take care of yourself."

Eddie wasn't sure if that was given as a warning, or just an everyday friendly remark.

Outside a black limousine stood parked in a bay on the small station forecourt. A man dressed in smart dark suit and peak cap waited beside it. Since only one other passenger had exited the station and already departed in a waiting car, the driver presumed this was Eddie, and beckoned him.

Eddie wondered for a moment if there was a mistake. Being invited to work at the consultant's home as a gardener, hardly warranted a chauffeur driven limousine, he thought. The driver detected his hesitation and called him by name.

"The surgeon's wife, Edith, has sent me to collect you," he said, opening the boot and placing his passenger's travel bag inside. Then he opened the rear door for him to enter. Eddie briefly glimpsed the man's face, but it was mostly hidden by the peak of his cap forming a shadow across the features.

"It's a three mile drive to the residence," he said in formal monotone, as if memorised in a collection of catchphrases for different occasions in his job.

Eddie settled back in the plush comfort of a soft black leather seat. A facing screen was set in the rear of the front seating, and a flap to the side, which Eddie pulled slightly open, revealed a small drinks cabinet. Luxury and wealth indeed, he thought, as the driver climbed in and set off.

The journey along a narrow lane took in further countryside, occasional gaps in tall hedgerows revealing more pastures.

Eventually the car turned into a narrower lane, soon arriving on the paved forecourt of what he presumed was their destination, Harcourt Grange.

Looming gloomily above its rural surrounds, a mansard roof crowned the three-storey, dark timber building, with a windowed attic room dominating the centre. Arched windows peered ominously down from the building, and a balustraded stairway rose to the covered entrance.

Eddie was impressed to say the least, but its imposing presence seemed to give him an uneasy feeling.

"Certainly a very grand house," Eddie attempted conversation as the chauffeur lifted the travel bag from the car boot and handed it to him. A nod was all he received. The driver climbed back into the vehicle and soon disappeared down a side driveway. Eddie presumed it was garaged somewhere at the rear, as he began climbing the entrance stairway.

A brass plate with Harcourt House embossed in black lettering was set in the sidewall by the front door. As he approached the door opened. A woman greeted him beaming a blush pink welcoming smile. Wavy honey coloured hair touched her shoulders. She wore a white, short sleeved blouse, wine red knee length skirt and dark red choker with an opal purple heart.

"You must be Eddie," she said. He put down the travel bag as she stepped forward in her black, low heeled suede shoes extending her hand to shake his. "Come on in," the woman moved aside to let him enter.

"I'm Edith Albright. Welcome to Harcourt House," she continued, now entering the spacious hall. Her chestnut brown eyes added warmth to her face, and Eddie found himself immediately attracted to the woman. She looked to be at least ten or more years younger than the mid fifties range Eddie had calculated for her husband.

As she spoke, an elderly grey-haired man appeared, wearing a white wing collared shirt, black bow tie, and dark suit with three silver buttons glistening each side of the jacket's wide lapels. Eddie thought he was dressed like someone out of the 19th century.

"This is Roberts our butler," Edith introduced him. "He'll take the travel bag to your room. In the meantime, I'm sure you'd like to take tea with me in the sitting room before freshening up for dinner." Eddie was not only sure he'd like to take tea with her, but absolutely certain.

Roberts took hold of the travel bag, glancing at its scuffed condition with disdain, and turned to make his way up the hall's broad, central wooden stairway.

Eddie paused for a moment, taking in the diamond shaped black and white floor tiles across the expanse of the hall. Several doors were spaced around the wood panelled setting, and clear glass globes with candlelight bulbs, stood poised on brass mounts for the hours of darkness.

As he turned to follow Edith through one of the doors, for a second he thought he saw his travel bag hovering in the air by itself near the top of the stairs. In the blink of an eye, he saw the butler, Roberts, holding it by the strap as he stepped on to the first floor landing. Eddie could have sworn he'd seen the bag moving without the butler's presence, but dismissed it as an optical illusion.

They entered the sitting room, an expansive setting with two floral patterned sofas facing a central coffee table. An oriental rug covered most of the room's highly polished wood flooring. On the panelled walls portraits of bearded men with stern expressions and austere looking women seemed to be staring in condemnation at him. It was a chilling greeting.

"Family members going back for generations," Edith informed him, noticing his interest. "And yes, they're a grim looking lot," she chuckled.

At the far end of the room a table and chairs were perched beside a window overlooking the forecourt below.

"Let's sit down," Edith beckoned him to the table, "our maid Betty will bring tea and biscuits shortly."

Eddie felt puzzled by his reception into the premises. A lowly employee being treated as if he was of some rank seemed strange. The house oozed wealth and a certain grandeur above the masses. It was not an unpleasant welcome, but he'd expected to be received at a tradesman's entrance.

"It looks a wonderful place," he said, taking a seat facing Edith, "have you lived here for long?" Eddie wondered if he should start probing the woman with questions, feeling a bit out of place as an employee.

"Oh, about ten years," she replied, not showing any objection to him asking. "The property has been in my husband Ernest's family for several generations. You've seen some of them in those portraits. His great, great, or is it three or four greats back, can never remember. Anyway, he made his fortune through a sideline business investment in tea importation back in the 18th century and bought this place."

She paused thoughtfully for a moment, as if trying to remember how many generations back it was, but decided not to pursue it.

"I met Ernest when I was working on a project at his hospital," she continued. "We just hit it off."

Eddie was about to ask her what work she'd been doing at the hospital, but was interrupted.

"Here's Betty with tea and biscuits," Edith caught sight of the maid approaching holding a silver tray. She was a young woman wearing a white sleeveless apron over a long black dress. A white mob cap rested on her auburn hair. She smiled nervously placing rose patterned bone china teaware and silvery cutlery on the table, as if demurring to important company. Then she gave curtsies to her mistress and guest before leaving the room.

"You seemed to be studying Betty's clothing," said Edith.

"I was," Eddie replied, "bit of a time throwback. Reminds me of photos I've seen of housemaids back a hundred years or so ago."

Edith smiled, as she rested the tea leaf strainer on his cup and began pouring from the teapot.

"Milk?"

Eddie nodded.

"Help yourself to sugar and biscuits," she gestured.

"My husband prefers to follow the traditional way of life in his family home," she began explaining. "He likes some of his staff to wear clothes that echo the past. The way they would have dressed back when his earlier ancestors lived."

Eddie thought it a little strange, but said nothing, accepting that within reason people could behave as they liked in their own homes.

"Of course, we won't expect you to dress like a gardener of the past. I don't think you have any intention to remain here as a permanent member of our staff," she assured.

The woman was right. He had no such intention. This was a temporary stop gap.

"I presume your husband told you about my hard luck story when he called you?" said Eddie, replacing his teacup in the saucer after taking a sip.

"I can assure you, I'm not sitting here in judgement," Edith replied. "Life takes us down many roads, often giving no clue to where they are leading. I had no idea coming from an ordinary family like my own, that I would end up being married to a brilliant surgeon and living in a magnificent house like this one."

"What surgery does your husband specialise in?" Eddie asked, intrigued to know. But he never received an answer.

At that moment a man entered the room and approached the table looking at Edith apologetically for the intrusion. He had swept back ginger hair, a slightly hooked nose, and briefly gave Eddie a glaring hawk like stare, as if ready to swoop on him.

Eddie took an instant dislike to the man, who was dressed in modern clothing of grey suit, blue shirt and navy tie. He guessed the arrival was in his early forties.

"I'm sorry to interrupt madam," he addressed Edith, "but cook is in a terrible mood about one of the kitchen staff, and I thought a word from you would calm things down."

"I know who you mean," Edith replied. "I think it's about time her presence here is terminated. Right Benson, I'll be there shortly." The man bowed and left the room.

"That's Joseph Benson, our estate general manager," she explained to Eddie. "Does an excellent job, but sometimes finds the female element a bit of a handful to manage." She stood up. "I'm sorry to leave you, but I'd better go and sort things out. Finish your tea, and Roberts the butler will come and show you to your room."

Eddie took another biscuit and sip of tea, wondering about the words she used to deal with the situation. He presumed 'it's about time her presence here is terminated', referred to the woman in the kitchen being dismissed from service. Yet the way Edith had delivered it seemed more ominous. He also wondered why the man Benson was in modern clothing unlike the other two employees he'd seen.

As he pondered these thoughts, a minute or so later Roberts the butler entered the room. He approached Eddie in a stiffly upright manner.

"Your room is now prepared," he announced formally. Eddie gulped down the remainder of his tea and followed the man out of the room.

As he climbed the hall stairway behind the butler, he wondered why Roberts' black patent leather shoes made no sound on the wooden steps. Eddie was in trainers, and soft soled as they were, they made at least a little. Surely leather shoes would sound louder. For a moment the memory returned of this man carrying his travel bag up the stairs on arrival. And those brief seconds when Roberts seemed to have disappeared while the bag continued to float upwards by itself.

Reaching the first floor landing with a corridor branching each way, Roberts led him to a room on the left side three doors down.

"I trust this will be in order for you Mr Cartwright," his stiff manner continued in his voice, making it sound more like a statement than an enquiry into satisfaction.

Since Eddie had spent the previous night sleeping on dirt in a park, anywhere with a roof over it was very satisfactory as far as he was concerned.

"I've taken the step to unpack your belongings and place them in the wardrobe and drawers," Roberts continued.

"Thank you," Eddie replied, a little annoyed the man had handled his meagre belongings without permission, but not enough to complain. The room didn't have the elegance of the fixtures and fittings he'd seen so far in the property. However, a comfortable single bed, bedside cabinet with light shade designed like an oil lamp, storage furniture and writing desk was all the luxury he needed. The adjoining en-suite was an added bonus.

"While unpacking I saw you possessed a rather worn pair of jeans and yellow T-shirt," the butler continued. "They will be perfectly suitable for your duties tomorrow. Dungarees will be provided for you."

Eddie considered it cheeky the man was commenting on the condition of his clothes, but couldn't disagree. They had seen better days, and he did have some better clothing he'd also packed, so he let it pass without comment.

"Dinner will be served at seven o'clock in the dining room," Roberts continued like an automaton. "Entry is in the hall. Take the door immediately to your left on descent." He made a slight bow, turned and left the room.

Eddie crossed to the floral curtained window overlooking the rear of the house. Below he could see a long sloping lawn spread with mature trees. In the distance fields and hedges stretched towards a hill lined horizon bathed in a blue grey haze.

To the left a cluster of trees surrounded what appeared to be a building, judging by a section of red tiled roof just visible through a small gap in branches. On the right, a low stone wall enclosed an expansive lawn containing numerous colourful flower beds.

Eddie's continuing sense of loss at parting from Steph still ran deep, but he was grateful of at least having a decent refuge in a beautiful setting. He looked at his watch. Nearly six o'clock. An hour to dinner. Eddie couldn't fathom being employed as a labourer, but so far being treated like a favoured guest. He wasn't complaining though.

Feeling tired after an eventful day of moving from homelessness to salvation, Eddie laid down on the bed for a short rest. Staring at the ceiling, he began to doze off when he heard a noise as if a chair had been scraped on the wood floor. He sat up and looked across at the writing desk chair. It appeared to have been turned a little sideways in the manner of someone beginning to pull it out to sit down.

Eddie felt certain it had been tucked into the desk footwell when he'd entered the room. Perhaps it was already pulled out a bit? In truth, he couldn't be certain.

He laid back on the bed feeling sleepy and began to doze again. It wasn't long before another chair scrape woke him. This time he sprung up hoping to catch someone sneaking about in the room. But there was no-one in sight, and he saw the chair was now tucked back into the desk.

Eddie wondered if there had been some ground tremors that he hadn't felt while dozing. It would be unusual for the tremors to move the chair out slightly then replace it again. But he was determined to look for a logical explanation.

Glancing at his watch, the time was now approaching six thirty, so he decided to freshen up for dinner.

CHAPTER 3

THE dining room was another wood panelled expanse. A variety of portraits depicting family groups dressed in clothes of past eras hung on the walls, along with paintings of countryside views and race horses.

A long, highly polished oak dining table spanned the centre, Georgian chairs lined the sides and ends, and a sparkling crystal chandelier gleamed above. A solitary silver cutlery place setting was laid at the entrance end, with a white folded napkin and silver condiment holders. Eddie presumed the setting was for him and sat.

Moments later the maid Betty entered through a side door and approached.

"The lady Edith sends her apologies," she began. "It was her intention to dine with you, but was called away on other duties." The woman appeared nervous, as if expecting a rebuke from Eddie for being stood up.

"I'd no idea she'd planned to eat with me," he replied," so no worries." The maid gave a smile of relief.

"The lady Edith chose a bottle of Château Mouton Rothschild vintage wine to go with your meal," Betty announced. From his experience in catering Eddie had some knowledge of wines, and although he was no expert, the variety chosen certainly came into the excellent range.

The choice of roast beef and vegetables or trout with either pasta, salad or butternut chilli was another option. Being a meat man, the choice for him was obvious. Steph would have enjoyed the other options. The thought made him sad, not having her by his side.

"I'll tell cook," said Betty and made for the side door entrance to the kitchen. Eddie blinked in disbelief for a second as he watched her leave. He was certain he'd seen her dissolve into thin air even as she was pushing open the door, but dismissed it as some sort of mirage.

As he waited for the meal, he studied the generations of family portraits. The expressions weren't as stern as the ones he'd seen in the sitting room. Formal but not forbidding. He assumed they had all been steeped in wealth, and now he was sampling a little of their luxurious lifestyles. Amazing his rise in fortune from the park bed to here in one day. Seemed a bit good to be true. A nagging doubt briefly clouded his mood.

Speedily it was driven away as Betty served the delicious meal and wine, and soon the food and alcohol warmed his soul. Strawberries and cream for dessert lifted his spirit even higher.

And then that annoying doubt returned. For a moment he compared himself to a condemned prisoner being given a favourite last meal before sentence was carried out.

Eddie picked up the jug of cream to pour another generous helping on the strawberries, then replaced it on the table. To his amazement, the jug suddenly rose unaided about four inches above the table and moved sideways a little, then descended as if returning itself to the exact spot where Betty had placed it when first serving the dessert.

Had he imagined it? Several glasses of the wine had given him a slightly woolly head, but he didn't consider himself drunk. He lifted the jug and placed it on a different spot. This time it remained there. He concluded the wine was more potent than he'd realised. Objects don't just lift themselves. He must have imagined it.

Betty returned to offer Eddie coffee, which he declined just as his hostess Edith entered the room. Betty curtsied in deference to her and left.

"So sorry not to join you this evening," she told Eddie, "but there were a few things I had to attend."

"No, no, it was a great meal and the wine was wonderful," Eddie reassured her.

"I'm pleased," Edith smiled. "I just came to tell you our head gardener, Bill Mason, will meet you at our greenhouse by the side of the house. We call him Mulch, because he's always going on about the importance of good compost for the plants," she laughed. Then she lifted the nearly empty wine bottle from the table to check the correct one had been served. Satisfied, she replaced it.

"Roberts says you have a T-shirt and jeans that look like they've seen better days," she continued. "Wear those for the gardening, and Mulch will supply you with dungarees and Wellington boots."

The reminder of the butler unpacking and commenting on his clothes annoyed Eddie, but he said nothing.

"He'll be expecting you at seven in the morning, so you better get a good night's sleep," Edith advised. "You'll only be on light duties, clearing weeds and some flower planting for now. Just enough to keep you in good condition. Breakfast will be served in here at six o'clock." She smiled and left.

Eddie thought about what she'd said. What did she mean about keeping him in good condition? An innocent and caring comment in its own right, but somehow it came across as having a loaded meaning. Good condition for what? Was there some other purpose for him?

Sunlight was edging towards its descent by the time Eddie left the dining room, and candlelight bulbs flickered in the glass globes as he entered the hall. In the dark wood panelled setting, they created a strong atmosphere of past eras, when oil lamps or real candles would have lit the way.

Eddie wobbled unsteadily from the effect of the wine as he made his way up the stairs, and held on to the bannister for support.

Reaching the landing he saw candlelights flickering in smaller glass globes, giving just enough illumination along the wood panelled corridor to see the way to his room. It looked a bit creepy he thought. All was quiet. Uncannily quiet, leaving him with the feeling he was the only person in the house.

Glancing at his watch, he saw it was nearly nine o'clock. He reasoned the emptiness was probably because all the staff, wherever they were in the house, probably all got up early and had already gone to bed.

Eddie entered his room and turned on the light. Three candlelight bulbs softly lit the room set in a cluster of clear, bell shaped shades hanging from an ornate ceiling rose. It bestowed a homely setting to the room, and the comfy looking bed almost seemed to cry out for him to rest.

Then his eyes caught sight of the writing table chair. He was certain it was tucked in before he left for dinner, but now it had been drawn much further out as if someone had been sitting on it.

Perhaps one of the staff, maybe a maid, had entered to check if the room needed attention while he'd been at dinner, and pulled out the chair for some reason. Whatever, he wasn't too bothered. And he certainly didn't have any valuable items that could make worthwhile gain for a thief. Just some loose change, which he noticed was still on the writing desk where he'd left it, along with some keys and a small framed photo of himself and Steph taken together in happier times. That was certainly valuable to him personally, though unlikely to accrue any income.

He still had a tidy sum of money in notes remaining from the generous donation given him by the surgeon for clothes and travel. But he kept that in his wallet, tucked in the back pocket of his trousers.

Eddie pushed the chair back into the desk, and in the same moment a thought came to him. In the top drawer where Roberts had placed his few possessions when unpacking, there should be his phone.

The events of arrival had distracted him from detail, and now he remembered he hadn't seen the phone. He opened the drawer and realised why. It was missing. He was certain he hadn't lost it, so why had it been removed? He'd ask Roberts tomorrow. For now the effect of draining nearly a bottle of vintage wine left him feeling exhausted.

Eddie paused before drawing the curtains of his bedroom window to glance outside. A sliver of cloud cut across the moon, but there was enough light to cast a silvery glow on the trees and grassy slope of the lawn. The peaceful view made him consider how lucky he'd been arriving at the house, with a job included.

After washing, he climbed into bed and turned off the bedside lamp. Darkness almost enclosed him. Moonlight slightly illuminated the room glowing through the closed curtains. Eddie soon fell asleep.

A LOUD scraping woke him, breaking the night stillness. He sat up sharply and leaned across, fumbling to turn on the bedside light.

Blinded for a second by the sudden brightness, he gazed round the room to see the chair he'd pushed back into the writing desk was now pulled out again. But other than himself the room was unoccupied. Eddie was determined that there was a logical explanation. A maid moving it while he was out at dinner was feasible. But now it had moved again while only he occupied the room.

For a few moments he was beginning to wonder if it was paranormal activity, some poltergeist. He shook his head. No. He felt stupid for even considering the notion. Of course there no such things as ghosts.

He decided since it was an old house, there was the greater possibility that aged foundations might shift now and again to cause the chair movement. He wasn't overly convinced by his own explanation, but that seemed more feasible than a spirit causing it. Satisfied with the thought, Eddie turned out the bedside lamp and settled down.

In the morning the chair remained in the same pulled out position, confirming his belief that nothing paranormal had been involved.

Dressed in jeans and T-shirt as suggested by the butler, Eddie descended the stairway to the dining room.

A choice of egg and bacon with toast or a grilled kipper was a hard call. He liked both, but opted for the fry up. It felt odd sitting at the long dining table as the only occupant of the room.

He imagined well heeled ancestors of the property holding dinners with guests dressed in their finery, the women wearing pearl and diamond necklaces, the men in expensive bespoke suits. The candelabra would glitter overhead, and exquisite food and wine would be served by an army of butlers and maids. Talk of investments, hunting, politics and fashion would have echoed round the room's expanse.

Presently the only echo was caused by the clunk of his knife and fork on the bone china plate, and clink of his teacup when he placed it on the saucer.

"Have you worked here long?" he asked the maid Betty as she returned to clear the breakfast things.

"Longer than I care to remember sir," she replied, a trace of weariness in her voice.

"Do you ever fancy a change?" Eddie pursued.

"Not so easy," she began, but was interrupted by Edith entering the room. Betty glanced nervously at her, as if expecting to be punished for talking with guests. Then she curtsied and hurriedly returned to the kitchen.

"Did you sleep well?" asked Edith. Eddie hesitated for a moment, wondering if he should mention the chair moving incident.

Perfectly well," he decided to answer, not wishing to risk her thinking he suffered from delusions.

"Good," she said, smiling. "Our head gardener Mulch knows you're only to be on light duties, so you shouldn't have too taxing a day."

"I wanted to ask," he began as she started turning to leave. "My phone is missing. I'm wondering if Roberts mislaid it when he was unpacking my things?"

Edith focused a resolute stare.

"We don't allow phones in the house or grounds," she announced firmly. "My husband is determined that as far as possible, we follow a traditional lifestyle here. It's difficult to live without some trappings of modernity in these times, but we like to keep them to a minimum."

The stern reply surprised Eddie.

"I hope you don't mind?" Edith's frosty manner swiftly softened, her tone changing to sound like a reasonable request.

"No, it's okay," he replied. There was no-one who would miss him not calling them, and he didn't want to risk being thrown out by objecting.

"I'm grateful." Her smile glowed superiority and she left.

As Eddie exited the room he was met by Roberts who'd just descended the staircase.

"The greenhouse can be reached along the corridor behind that door," he pointed to it at the far end of the hall to the left side of the stairway.

The corridor led to another door opening to the rear of the property. He stepped on to a gravelled stretch and saw a fabulous widespread lawn with numerous circular beds stocked with vividly colourful flowers.

A wide gravelled path ran between the setting, and at the far end a white marble angel, with wings spread wide, spouted water from its mouth into the pool below. Eddie stood admiring the view.

"You must be our new recruit," a voice interrupted the peaceful moment. Eddie turned to see a heavily built man wearing a black waistcoat over a white shirt with rolled up sleeves. His buff trousers and brown boots were streaked with dry mud.

"I'm Mulch the head gardener," he introduced himself, extending a soil strewn handshake. The grip almost crushed Eddie's.

"Yes, I'm the new recruit," he winced in pain, greeting the middle-aged leathery face gazing at him, which appeared to be assessing his suitability for gardening. The man released him from the vice like grip.

"The lady Edith says you're only to do light duties for now, so come to the garden shed by the greenhouse and we'll kit you in dungaree and boots," Mulch boomed in a deep voice.

Eddie followed the man entering the large shed containing an assortment of shovels and garden forks resting on one side. Shelves above were stacked with plant trays and smaller gardening tools. On the other side, hooks held dungarees with a selection of Wellington boots in a row below.

After finding suitable sizes for Eddie, the head gardener led him to one of the circular flower beds on the lawn which needed planting up, along with a few others nearby. Several gardeners were tending to flowers in bloom a little further away. Mulch pointed Eddie to a small garden fork, shovel and seedlings in plant trays resting nearby.

"It's not strenuous work planting them up, so even someone with your pale town dweller face should be able to cope," Mulch laughed, shaking his head. Eddie ignored the remark, seeing no point in showing offence. He had a valuable refuge for now, and once again would take no chance on being thrown out. Eddie began his work placing the plants where Mulch had directed before leaving.

After planting a dozen from the trays, he stood up to stretch his back and turned to gaze across the lawn for a minute. When he turned back to resume, he saw several plants had been unearthed and tossed aside.

Annoyed, he looked around to see who might be the suspect. The other gardeners were too far off for Eddie not to have heard or noticed any of them approaching. Whoever had done it must have been able to move like a sprite, he thought. Surely he would have detected some movement, heard a sound from someone who would need to be so close to him.

As he stooped to start replanting the uprooted ones, Mulch seemed to appear from nowhere next to him.

"Had an argument with them?" he asked wryly. Eddie stood up to face his boss.

"Someone just pulled them out while I wasn't looking," he said. "Must have moved like the wind. I didn't see or hear anything."

A smile rose on Mulch's face.

"I think you'll find it was that little imp, Jeremiah," he replied. Eddie gazed at him mystified.

"He's a ten-year-old boy," Mulch explained. "Causes a lot of mischief around the house."

"Is he the Albright's son?" asked Eddie. The gardener laughed.

"No, he's just a street urchin. The Albright's saved him and his father after they were run down by a Hansom cab. Been a nuisance both of them ever since."

Eddie was totally phased. A Hansom cab? They were horse drawn carriages used over a century ago, but not now. The gardener must have had some sort of mind slip. Perhaps he liked reading historical books and mixed it up with a minicab or taxi.

"He needs a good clip round the ear," growled Mulch, and stooped down to help Eddie replant before leaving for another task. The assistance caused Eddie to raise his opinion of the man, deciding that Mulch's earlier rude description of him was just a rough side to his otherwise decent character.

After planting up more flower beds and weeding several others on Mulch's instruction, the head gardener came to fetch him for the lunch break. He was provided with a plastic box containing ham sandwiches, crisps, an apple, and orange juice.

He sat eating alone on a bench beside the shed, facing a waist height hedge about ten feet beyond the gravel surface. Suddenly Eddie nearly choked eating a crisp. A pair of shears appeared, trimming top growth on the hedge in front of him without anyone operating them. For a few moments Eddie stared wide eyed at the strange spectacle, then the upper half of a fair-haired young man appeared behind the hedge working them.

Eddie shook his head in confusion. He seemed to be seeing a lot of weird events at the place. Was he starting to suffer delusions of the mind, he wondered? The trimmer paused for a moment and smiled a greeting, then continued his work remaining visible.

Eddie recalled the moving chair in his room. The jug of cream on the dining room table levitating. His travel bag seeming to travel by itself for a second as Roberts briefly disappeared carrying it up the stairs. And Betty looking as though she was dissolving, pushing open the kitchen door. Perhaps it was his own senses causing imaginary events. His thoughts were interrupted by Mulch arriving to give him afternoon duties.

By the end of the day, Eddie ached all over. He wasn't unfit, just that he'd been using muscles and ligaments unaccustomed to gardening postures.

Back in his room, he found he'd been supplied with new clothes in the wardrobe, a couple of white shirts, a black suit and a dark blue patterned tie. The clothing appeared to be his size. As he studied the additions, a knock came at the door. Opening it, Eddie saw the butler stiffly standing there.

"The lady Edith has requested you wear the clothing I've taken the liberty to place in your wardrobe," he announced. "She wishes you to dress smartly for dinner in the evenings."

Eddie did think the intrusion and command was a liberty, but again did not wish to offend the household.

"As the lady wishes," Eddie replied, mimicking Roberts' stuffy tone in a mocking response. But the sarcasm appeared to go over the butler's head. He left and Eddie closed the door.

Someone must have taken his measurements from his other clothing to buy the new ones in his size. Another intrusion. Probably a maid.

At dinner, freshened up and feeling uncomfortable in the formal wear, he found himself sitting alone again.

"Why am I dining in here?" he asked Betty when she came to take his order. "Why am I not eating with the other staff employed here?"

"Well the new ones always do," she replied.

"New ones?" Eddie asked in surprise. "What do you mean?"

"That's not for me to answer sir," the maid grew nervous.

"Where do the rest of the staff eat?" Eddie couldn't let it go.

"At one time it was in the kitchen downstairs sir," Betty replied.

"At one time? What do you mean?" he continued to press. Now the maid was looking extremely nervous.

"I shouldn't be saying sir," came her hesitant reply.

"Where is the kitchen downstairs?" Eddie insisted, not wishing to distress her further, but desperate to get to the bottom of this enigmatic exchange. The secrecy was beginning to bother him, coupled with the strange sights he had witnessed. Maybe he hadn't been imagining them. There was something distinctly odd going on.

"There's a back entrance for the staff dining area, but it can also be reached from the inside by a door in the hall under the stairs." The words came out in a flurry, as if she felt the need to let him know, but regretted saying them as quickly as they'd been delivered. That moment the dining room door opened.

"Why aren't you going about your duties?" Edith demanded sharply.

"Sorry ma'am," Betsy curtsied with a look of terror, then took Eddie's food order from the choice she gave, and swiftly left for the kitchen. Edith's sour expression followed the maid's departure, and transformed into a smile as she turned to the lone diner.

"I'm sorry you're being bothered by the maid," she apologised. "She's an absolute treasure in her work, but not a little scatter brained."

"We were just having a chat," said Eddie. "Probably my fault for distracting her." He didn't want Betty to be in any trouble. Edith ignored his remark.

"I came to see how you got on today," she changed the subject.

"Fine. Aching a bit after planting heaven knows how many beds, but it wasn't too taxing," he answered.

"Good." Edith looked across the expanse of the dining room. "I keep meaning to join you for dinner. Must feel lonely eating in this big room alone," she sympathised. "Things keep cropping up though, preventing me from dining with you. I hope you don't mind."

"Well no. But it would be good to have some company," Eddie replied. He paused. "I'm just wondering why I seem to be honoured with dining in this elegant setting, and not eating with your other employees. Mulch told me they all stay out the house."

Edith's gaze seemed to grow distant for a moment, as if her mind was busily calculating.

"You're not really a permanent member of our staff, so I thought you'd prefer not to mix in their rough and ready company." Edith's reply didn't quite ring as the absolute truth, Eddie felt.

"Well, I'm not exactly high class myself," he said. "I wouldn't mind dining with them. Betty said something about the staff at one time eating in the kitchen downstairs. In the basement I presume."

Edith momentarily bristled. He detected the woman was annoyed by his comment, and of what Betty had revealed to him.

"I'd rather you didn't join them for now," she responded icily. "There'll be time for that. Now just enjoy your meal."

Eddie did enjoy his meal. Expertly cooked trout, chocolate torte dessert and another bottle of fine wine, from which he could only manage a couple of glasses before his head began to swim a little.

Throughout the meal he continued to mull over Edith's words about dining with the staff. In particular, *'I'd rather you didn't join them for now. There'll be time for that.'*

If Edith looked on him as not being a permanent member of staff, her words now tended to imply there was a likelihood he might be one later. He'd given no indication that is what he wished. What was really in her mind? Eddie began to wonder why he'd been offered refuge here?

The meal and the wine after his day's work made him feel sleepy. Bed beckoned for a good night's rest before his early start in the morning. Settled under the comfort of the quilt, sleep quickly followed.

A scrape of the desk chair woke him.

"Is that you Jeremiah?" he called out, remembering Mulch telling him about the unseen mischievous ten-year-old boy, who he suspected had uprooted the flower bed plants.

As Eddie reached out to switch on the bedside lamp and reveal the culprit, a youngster's cheeky laugh broke out. The light came on, but no-one else was in sight. The boy surely couldn't have escaped through the door in that time?

Eddie climbed out of bed and opened it, looking both ways along the dimly lit corridor. There was no-one to be seen outside.

Mystified he closed the door, gazing round the room, checking under the bed and in the wardrobe without seeing anyone.

He pushed the chair back into the desk foot-well, still puzzling over how the boy could have escaped without sight or sound. He didn't want to consider the possibility that only the paranormal activity of a ghost could provide an explanation. But he couldn't help his mind wandering to the other strange phenomena he'd experienced.

"Ridiculous," he assured himself out loud. "Not possible." He got back into bed desperately trying to calculate how the chair and other odd events seemingly happened without human aid.

Magicians, he thought, could pull off tricks that seemed impossible, so weird sights of this kind could happen. But there were no magicians he was aware of staying at the property, and if there were, why would they waste time playing tricks like this on him?

As he gradually drifted into sleep, Eddie had the sensation of falling towards a giant sticky web before tiredness overtook him.

CHAPTER 4

NEXT morning Mulch set him to work in the greenhouse. Long shelves on both sides of the large structure contained many varieties of young plants in trays at different stages of growth.

Eddie's job was to remove the ones ready for outside planting and replace them in trays to be carried to the flower beds.

His skills at prising them out with a small scoop was not exactly expert, and a couple of hours later when Mulch returned to the greenhouse, he shook his head in dismay.

"I think you'd be better employed at just digging trenches for potato planting," he observed.

Eddie couldn't argue with the man's verdict, given he'd managed to crush a number of the plants clumsily transferring them.

"Pity I can't give you a digging job tomorrow," Mulch continued regretfully, "but the lady Edith has given me orders just to keep you on light duties. He shook his head again. "And you can't get much lighter gardening work than transferring young plants from one tray to another." The man wandered off, mumbling what sounded like unpleasant descriptions of his employee.

EDDIE sat in the dining room dressed in his new evening wear, when a different maid entered from the kitchen. She looked middle-aged and well built, approaching him grim faced, unlike the smiling Betty.

Dark brown hair with grey tinges protruded below her mob cap. The woman glowered at him from her aggressive, square jaw face as she stood beside the table to take his order.

"Where's Betty?" asked Eddie.

"On other duties," she curtly replied.

Eddie was about to ask which other duties, but decided this maid was unlikely to engage in social conversation. She blurted out the food on offer and left with his order.

When it arrived, the woman dumped the plate heavily on the table out of one hand, followed by similar unceremonious delivery of a water jug from the other. Eddie noted no wine was being served on this occasion.

As the maid returned to the kitchen, Eddie had the distinct feeling that he'd done something to upset Edith. His less than expert gardening efforts earlier that day could hardly have been a reason to ruffle her feathers. If Mulch had told her about his clumsiness, she'd likely to have told him not to bother her with such trivial matters. No, Eddie sensed it may have been more to do with the conversations he had with Betty.

On both occasions when the maid was starting to engage with him, Edith had the uncanny knack of entering the room. It was obvious she was displeased with her servants engaging with him on matters not relating to his dining requirements.

She'd glared frostily at Betty just after the maid had told him about staff eating in a basement kitchen. She must have heard Betty from outside the door. As he ate the meal, his desire to investigate the basement dining area grew.

After finishing dinner, Eddie returned to his room determined to wait a few hours until everyone would likely have gone to bed. He'd brought a mystery thriller book to read, and settled on his bed to pass the time. At nearly midnight, he decided to embark on his mission, feeling confident everyone would have settled down by now.

It was difficult for him to assess who might be residing in the house, not knowing whether the servants had rooms in it too, or separate living quarters elsewhere in the grounds. Whichever, caution was the keyword.

The dimly glowing glass globes on the walls provided enough light for Eddie to find his way down the stairway. Occasional creaks from the wooden steps echoed across the spacious hall, causing him to stop and listen for a moment in case it alerted someone. Satisfied no-one had heard him, at the bottom he tiptoed his way across to the door under the stairway that Betty told him led to the servants dining room.

Gripping the handle he carefully opened the door. The low lighting in the hall now provided even less illumination for penetrating the darkness inside, but his eyes swiftly adjusted to the lower level, so that he could make his way in the narrow passageway ahead.

Then he caught sight of a switch on the wall to his left. He flicked it, hoping it connected to a working bulb. It did. The light came from a single bulb attached to a flex from the ceiling. It was dim, but now brighter for him to see the way.

At the end of the passage, which he estimated to be about 20 feet, there were openings to the left and right. The end of the corridors on both sides led to arched wooden doors.

Eddie chose the left side to examine first. The circular, black door handle was slightly rusted, but with a squeak opened when turned. Inside, the diminished corridor light showed a flight of steps descending to another arched door. The brass circular door handle was even more rusted, grinding as he turned it.

He expected to find whatever lay behind to be in complete darkness, and was surprised to see moonlight shining through a long window on his left as he entered the room. In the silvery glow, he could make out a flight of steps outside the window leading down to a small paved area giving door access into the room. Eddie wondered if it was the servants' entrance.

Now in the moon glow, he could see a long bench table, a metal cooking range, pots and pans on shelves and a stone sink. All had coatings of cobwebs and thick dust. Was this the staff dining area Betty had referred to? It was obvious the setting hadn't been used for many years. How long had she been working here to know this setting when it was in use? And where did she eat now?

Eddie saw another door beside the cooking range and approached, pressing his thumb down on a latch to open it.

"What are you doing here?" a voice shot from behind.

Eddie swung round to see Joseph Benson, the estate manager, who he'd briefly met when taking tea with Edith on arrival. The man stood by the entrance door casting an unfriendly glare at him, made all the more menacing by the shadowy contours of his face in the moonlight. He seemed to have arrived without a sound, as if materialising on the spot.

"I...I..." Eddie was stuck for an excuse.

Benson continued to stare, appearing to relish Eddie's embarrassed discomfort.

"You shouldn't be here," Benson growled, when satisfied Eddie had suffered enough uneasiness. He wasn't interested in hearing some pathetic excuse for the intrusion.

"Please return to your room." The man's tone conveyed an order rather than a request.

"Benson turned and mounted the steps followed by Eddie. In the hall he gave another glowering stare, and watched as Eddie ascended the stairway to his room, making him feel like a schoolboy who'd just been caught breaking school rules by teacher. Approaching his bedroom, Eddie felt there was something nasty and evil about the man, and considered it best to avoid confrontation with him as far as possible.

When he climbed into bed, it took a while for him to settle, his nerves jarred by the encounter. Okay, so it was a disused dusty room he'd visited, but he perceived Benson and Edith were unsettled by him gaining any knowledge about the property beyond a certain point. Yes, he shouldn't have been snooping, however, Benson's terse manner seemed to contain a warning far beyond what would have been necessary in asking him to leave.

Eddie felt the urge to investigate further another time. There was something far more than just a dusty old room that they didn't want him to see. Of that he felt certain. Only next time he'd take more care to ensure he wasn't being followed. Sleep gradually came to him, but it was an unsettled night's rest.

"RIGHT, I want you to clean and grease garden tools today," Mulch gave his order standing outside the greenhouse, wiping soil off his hands with an old rag.

The man led him to a paved area beside the greenhouse, where a selection of garden tools, loppers, edgers, shears, pruners, and many more than Eddie could ever have imagined existed, were laid in rows. He was given rags to clean them and a large pot of grease for their lubrication.

By the end of the day his hands were painfully sore, ingrained with soil, and on several occasions he'd narrowly missed slicing his fingers on razor sharp blades. It reinforced his belief that professional gardening was not a career path he intended to pursue.

That evening, the grim maid who'd replaced Betty brought no cheer to the dining room, remaining sullenly silent when he tried to strike up conversation. After eating, he was preparing to leave when Edith entered the room and seated herself opposite him at the table.

"Did you enjoy your meal?" she asked amiably.

"Excellent," Eddie replied, genuinely impressed by the quality of the food.

"Good," Edith smiled. "We like to make people staying here feel at home," she said, pausing briefly. "But we also like people to respect our home."

Eddie could feel there was a barb coming, hidden in the woman's polite introduction.

"That means they should not wander into places where they haven't been invited," she added sternly.

Benson had apparently told her of his visit to the basement last night. Eddie was about to apologise for the incident, but Edith raised her hand, anticipating he was planning a response.

"I think nothing more should be said about it," she commanded. "I'm sure we both understand each other." The woman stood up. "I hope you have a pleasant night." Edith gave a curt smile and left the room.

Like the night before in Benson's presence, Eddie felt like a diminished schoolboy receiving a warning for misbehaviour. If Eddie was going to explore the house further, he'd have to be much more careful.

WITH the onset of twilight approaching, after dinner Eddie decided to go for a stroll on the sloping lawn he'd seen from his bedroom window. As yet his daily labours hadn't taken him to this part of the estate, and he was keen to explore a little further before darkness enclosed the setting.

He rounded the greenhouse at the side of the house and reached a wide paved area along the rear line of the property. From here he began descending the slight incline of the lawn, which steepened as he progressed, and the view of the house behind gradually disappeared from view.

At the bottom a stream trickled past, forming the lawn's boundary. The other side of the water was covered by a line of tall bushes. Eddie thought he could go no further, when he caught sight of a narrow wooden footbridge straddling the stream a short distance to the left.

He crossed the bridge and saw a footpath leading from it, which was bounded by more tall bushes. After about twenty feet, the view opened on to a field dotted with trees. The path continued along the left side of the field, soon to be swallowed by yet another cluster of bushes.

This time the path opened to reveal a large brick building with a flat concrete roof, on a lawn surrounded by high bushes. The well hidden structure was completely out of keeping with the elegance of the main house and other settings he'd seen so far on the estate.

A broad, metallic tube rose from the centre of the roof, which Eddie presumed was a chimney.

He approached the structure, puzzling as to its use. Burning things was the likely answer, but it seemed a long way from the precincts of the house to be of practical access. On the other hand, it might be used to burn tree and bush cuttings further from the house, he decided.

A paved pathway ran around the building, which was fronted by a sturdy, black metal front door. On each side of the structure, three small frosted square windows were set about ten feet high in the brown brickwork, just below the roofline.

There was handle on the door above a large keyhole. Eddie tried to open it in the hope it might be unlocked, but the barrier didn't budge. The windows were too high for viewing inside, and the frosting probably wouldn't provide an insight anyway.

Daylight had now begun to fade, and he decided to return to the house. As he started to leave, a man's voice came from behind.

"In case you're wondering, they do burn things in there, but not only wood or chopped bushes," he said.

Eddie turned to see a man with a greying black beard, wearing a flat cap, collarless shirt with dark red neckerchief, and grey trousers supported by braces. Lines furrowed his brow, and his eyes carried a glint of curiosity. For some reason, the figure reminded Eddie of a labourer from a past era.

"If I was you," the man continued in a London accent, "I'd get away from this place as soon as you can. Your life's in danger," he warned.

Eddie stood transfixed, not knowing if an apparition had just appeared, or if he was a living being.

"Someone from the house is coming to find you. There's eyes and ears all over the place where you're staying." The man seemed to be detecting something not yet in sight.

"Come back another time if you haven't been able to get away from here, and I'll tell you what's going on. I'm always around." The man disappeared into thin air.

Eddie's jaw dropped. Had what he'd seen and heard actually happened? If so, he'd just seen a ghost. The warning of his life being in danger shocked him. He knew Harcourt Grange was turning out to be a strange place....but his life threatened?

Feeling bewildered, he began to make his way back along the footpath, the sky now rapidly fading into twilight. As he crossed the wooden footbridge, he was met by the figure of Benson standing on the other side. The person, or phantom, Eddie had seen was right. Someone was coming his way.

"You could lose your way wandering around the estate in the darkness," said Benson as Eddie reached him, sounding as if he was concerned for the newcomer's welfare. "Best be getting back now."

Eddie fell for a moment into believing the man cared for his welfare, but it didn't fit with his experience of him so far. He felt like a helpless pawn in a game he didn't understand.

Not another word passed between them as Benson, fixed in rigid upright posture and stern gaze, gave the impression of escorting rather than accompanying Eddie back to the house.

THE SPECTRE at the building in the clearing pervaded Eddie's thoughts as he got ready for bed and settled to rest.

Dr Albright's generous offer of temporary refuge at Harcourt Grange was dramatically not turning out as he'd anticipated. Though unsettling, he was prepared to endure the strange occurrences that had manifested. But now the blatant appearance of an apparition to warn him he was in danger. That went further than being unsettling. It was deeply disturbing.

On the other hand, had he really seen a ghost? Was it some estate worker playing a joke on him? As he lay in bed, he considered the possibility. The man could have slipped round the corner of the building to appear at the entrance door. Eddie had been in the process of turning his back to return to the house, when he'd heard the voice from behind.

However, what confounded the theory of it being a human was the fact he'd disappeared into the air. It would need some accomplished conjuring act to create that illusion.

Perhaps it was time to disappear quietly from the house himself, Eddie decided. He still had a reasonable amount of money left from the donation Albright had given him. Enough at least to to survive for several days while working out a plan to get by, or find some casual work. Right now the imperative to escape took precedence over fine detail of future prospects.

Tomorrow would be Friday, another day of tedious gardening chores as Eddie had come to view them. But Saturday was a half day. He could use the afternoon to escape. He'd considered night as a possibility, but would likely end up hopelessly lost in darkness in a countryside area he didn't know. Now satisfied with positive thought of escaping, he settled to sleep.

CHAPTER 5

SITTING on the bench beside the greenhouse, Eddie finished his packed lunch sandwiches provided by the kitchen. It was the end of Saturday morning's gardening chores, and he'd been considering how he could escape from Harcourt Grange since rising.

The railway station was miles away, and he had no idea how to get there. The car that had brought him to the house took several turns along the way, confusing his memory of the route.

He'd decided he would take a walk towards distant fields until he came across some place where he could seek directions to transport. If he had to sleep rough somewhere on the way, so be it. He'd experienced that anyway, and it would be far safer than staying in a house where his life could be in danger, or where some other strange encounter might confront him.

Eddie discarded his dungarees in the nearby storeroom, and patted the back pocket of his trousers to ensure the wallet was still there. It would look suspicious if he was seen trying to leave with his travel bag. Possessions, meagre as they were, would have to be left behind.

He chose to leave by a direction he'd seen during his gardening work on the opposite side of the ornate flower garden.

No-one was in sight as he made his way along the rear of the house, arriving at the narrow side road leading from the forecourt. Further down it curved into a gap between high hedgerows. Eddie walked down the tarmac route, sauntering as if he was just taking a stroll, rather than looking for a suitable exit from the place.

As the road curved further round, a single storey, yellow brick building with a pitched slate roof came into view, fronted by three up-and-over doors. On a small forecourt in front, Eddie spied the limousine that had brought him here from the station. For a second he feared the driver might be nearby and wonder why he was there. Eddie wanted his escape route to go undetected.

Gazing around he could see no-one was about, and with great relief reached the garage forecourt. From here he could see a field behind the garage sloping away into the distance, gradually disappearing from view.

Eddie began his trek across the field with no idea where it might lead, only that his route must eventually arrive at a house, farm or village, where he could ask for use of a phone to book a cab to the nearest station.

He glanced back while descending the sloping field to catch a glimpse of the top floor windows of Harcourt Grange disappearing from view. A line of trees had helped obscure lower window views of the route. Now at last he was completely out of sight.

At the bottom of the field, Eddie approached a stream. On the other side was an upward sloping field. The clear flowing water between wasn't deep, and only about ten feet wide, but no stepping stones were in sight, and his trainers and socks became soaked as he waded across. No matter, a small price to pay to escape from the wretched place.

So far all had been well. Several times he'd glanced back to make sure he wasn't being followed. But seeing no pursuer, a feeling of being watched gradually subsided.

Reaching the top of his climb on the other side of the stream, a clear view of distant fields and woodland appeared. From his high vantage point he could see a village nestled in the valley below, highlighted by a turreted church tower with clusters of nearby cottages.

His spirit soared. Now he began heading towards it, certain he could make a swift escape by hiring a cab there to the station.

Descent was reasonably straightforward, with slight detours needed along the edge of fields where crops were planted. In the last field, what looked like a bull was grazing. Its interest in him prompted the animal to begin swiftly trotting towards him, causing Eddie to break into a run for a wooden gate and rapidly climb over. He landed on a grass verge bordering a narrow lane, which looked like it led in the direction of the village.

Soon he reached the high street with shops on each side. Passing shoppers lifted his spirit even further, as he sampled the familiarity of mixing with outside human life. A little further along he saw the stone wall frontage and lychgate entrance to the turreted church he'd first viewed from the hilltop. Not far ahead he could now seen a pub called The Royal Oak, featuring a tree image on a hoarding above the inn's entrance.

The building had lichen dotted liberally on the granite stone frontage. Slate roof tiles, continued nature's theme of lichen, and the leaded light front windows, sat comfortably with these obvious signs of age. Eddie felt in need of refreshment and made his way into the premises.

Customers seated at tables turned their heads to briefly look at the newcomer, before resuming their conversations. A broad brick fireplace dominated one end of the pub with recesses each side. In colder months Eddie could imagine a warming log fire burning in the hearth, keeping the setting warm and cosy. Dark oak beams on the ceiling and walls, boasted the inn's 18th century age.

Eddie approached the bar, where two customers stood chatting at one end with beers in hand. The barman, a young man with neatly trimmed black hair, stubble beard and red open neck shirt, smiled at him as he reached the counter.

"Afternoon," he greeted.

Eddie returned the smile and ordered a beer. He felt greatly relieved to be back in a place where everything appeared relaxed and normal, unlike the strange setting he'd just left.

The barman placed the pint of ale on the bar, and Eddie paid from some of the remaining money Dr Albright had given him. At the same time he ordered a round of ham sandwiches offered on the chalked menu board behind the bar.

"Can I call a cab from here?" he asked the barman, who indicated a notice board with cab business cards, dates of darts matches at the inn, and local sports fixtures attached to it.

"I've lost my phone," said Eddie, seeing the inn had no payphone, and realising the barman expected him to have one. "Could I possibly use yours?" he pleaded.

The young man eyed Eddie suspiciously. A stranger suddenly appearing and asking to use his personal possession. The barman wavered, mentally weighing him up.

"You can dial the cab number. I'm not trying to run off with it or make some premium price call," Eddie attempted to assure him. "It's just that I've lost my phone," he persisted. The man behind the bar still wavered.

"I've been on a hike and lost it somewhere on the way. I need to reach the nearest train station so I can get home." Eddie embroidered the scenario. He had hiked and *lost* possession of his phone, but didn't want to explain true reasons why, or give any connection with Harcourt Grange.

Warily the man reached for his phone on the shelf behind the bar and handed it to Eddie. He stepped across to choose a cab hire number from a card on the notice board, and began to call. The inn door suddenly swung open to reveal his spy tormentor Benson entering and surveying the scene.

The customers stopped talking, detecting a sense hostility from the new arrival now focused on Eddie, who lowered the phone as a voice on the other end began speaking. Benson approached him, indicating he wanted the phone. Eddie handed it to him, mesmerised like a rabbit caught in car headlights.

"That's my phone!" the barman protested.

Benson placed it on the counter, ignoring the man as if he didn't exist.

"Time for us to go," the surly estate manager ordered, twisting Eddie's arm behind his back.

As he conducted him towards the door, he stopped.

"This man has escaped from a mental health facility," Benson announced to the inn customers. "I've been tracking him for days, and am now taking him back."

Everyone stared aghast, as Benson escorted him out.

Eddie was stunned, trying to take in the sudden turn of events. Even if he protested, now tainted as someone so mentally afflicted he needed retrieving, cries for help would sound hollow.

Benson led him to the car parked on the road outside, hand still firmly gripping Eddie's arm. As the man opened the back door to usher him inside the vehicle, his vice like grip loosened a little. It was enough for Eddie to free himself.

In an instant he was belting down the road. He briefly glanced back, anticipating Benson in pursuit, but his would be captor was nowhere to be seen. Had he jumped in the car to give pursuit?

A wood lay a short distance beyond the road's grass verge. The car wouldn't be able to follow him in there. He could hide himself among the trees and undergrowth. He veered towards it, and was about to disappear in the wood, when Benson appeared just a few feet in front of him."

"You can't escape," he snarled. Eddie jolted to a halt. It was impossible that the man could have reached the spot before him. Surely? He'd have needed to be an Olympic sprinter, or possess some unearthly power of travel. Even knowing a short cut seemed improbable.

"Wherever you go, I can arrive there faster," said Benson. In the same moment he disappeared into thin air.

Eddie stared agape. A few seconds later a voice came from behind.

"I'm here now."

Eddie swung round. Benson stood with a wicked smile on his face. Eddie continued to stare in shock.

It was dawning on him that the man was in fact a ghost. A poltergeist able to manipulate solid material as if a living being. Now Eddie was totally stunned, beginning to wonder if all the staff at Harcourt Grange might be ghosts.

The strange chair scrapes and movement in his room. The plants that had been unearthed when he was gardening. Mulch told him it was a mischievous boy named Jeremiah. Was the youngster a ghost? Was Mulch a ghost?

Eddie's skin began to creep, but he was in such a deep state of shock and confusion, he couldn't resist the powerful grip on his arm again, as the other world incarnation led him back to the car.

CHAPTER 6

BACK in his room Eddie's stupor continued to possess him. His mind still struggled to come to terms with the bizarre dilemma, which seemed impossibly possible.

Was he in some horrific coma? Had he been the victim of an accident that now left him insensible to the real world?

Through the night he remained in the stupor, laying on his bed fully clothed and for most of the following day, drifting in and out of confused sleep. His disappointment at not escaping added to the depression, fearing he would never be able to leave the place.

By evening the following day, the sense of his surroundings began to return. No, he was not in a coma, but he *was* in a complete mess.

For some reason he was being held as a prisoner. For what? Now Eddie reasoned the man he'd seen the other evening, when he'd come across that building on his walk, was also a ghost.

The warning from him that his life was in danger, now seemed to be a reinforced possibility. But what form of danger? After resting and rationalising his position, Eddie's fighting spirit had returned, and now it was imperative for him to escape, and not wait to find out.

However, in the face of ghosts with mighty supernatural powers as demonstrated by Benson, it would not be easy.

Eddie raised himself from the bed, feeling as though he was coated in a layer of dust, unwashed, with stubble on his face, and clothes smelling of dried sweat from his trek.

Showering, shaving and finding fresh clothes in the wardrobe, he made his way down to the dining room, though not feeling hungry. He was hoping Edith would come in as she had several times before. He wasn't sure any food would have been prepared for him, but that didn't matter. A meeting with Edith was all he desired.

Entering the dining room, he heard the sound of clattering and conversation coming from the kitchen. Curious to see inside, Eddie approached the door and pushed it open.

Peering inside, he stiffened in amazement to see pots, pans and crockery moving about as if a meal was being prepared, levitating without anyone visible manipulating it.

The room was a mixture of ancient and modern. An old, black metal range with steam rising from a saucepan, stone sink, a flaking ceiling, fowl hanging from hooks, and a deeply scored, wood food preparation table in the centre. But on an old chest of drawers stood a microwave and electric kettle.

As he backed out of the kitchen from shock, he was confronted by the surly maid who'd replaced Betty. She stared at him aggressively.

"Guests and workers are not allowed in the kitchen without permission," she fired at him.

Eddie was taken aback for a second by the woman's rudeness. Then anger struck him.

"Do not tell me what I should and shouldn't do. I don't answer to you," Eddie vented his fury. "You're probably a bloody ghost anyway!"

The maid stood resolutely defiant. Eddie wasn't sure if she was actually a spirit or a living person. The puzzle remained unanswered. Next moment Edith entered the room.

"Is there a problem?" she asked, seeing Eddie and the maid eyeing each other with intense dislike. Eddie swung round to face Edith approaching from the doorway.

"Yes there is a bloody problem," shouted Eddie. "Why am I being held a prisoner here?"

Edith remained unphased, dismissing the maid with a flick of her hand to go into the kitchen.

"Come and sit down," she invited him calmly, going over to the dining table and pulling out a chair for him, then seating herself on one opposite. Her calm conduct softened his anger a little, but he still simmered inside. With the unfriendly maid gone, he accepted the invitation and joined her.

"Benson told me what happened, and I'm sorry you're so upset," Edith began her explanation.

Eddie's jaw dropped. The woman's apology seemed to make it sound like a trivial incident being forcibly returned to the house. He was about to voice his protest, but she continued, ignoring the astonishment in his face.

"You see my husband wishes to show you some very interesting research he's working on," she said. "He believes you may be able to make a valuable contribution to it." She gave Eddie a warm smile. "It could lead you to becoming involved in medical advancements, and give you a whole new start."

"What research? How could it help me?" Eddie was interested, but not wholly sure without more detail.

"My husband wants to explain it to you in person," she replied. "He thinks that when I explain, I miss out some important points that are crucial to the overall picture." She beamed another smile. Eddie felt none the wiser.

"He's tied up at the hospital right now," she continued "but he says he'll be coming here in a few days or so. I'll let you know."

"That still doesn't explain why I've been forcibly made to stay here," Eddie was not prepared to let her off the hook so easily.

"Well, if you'd like to return the rest of the money my husband gave to you, and make your way without a penny, okay." Edith replied. "My husband offered you help in good faith, and you betrayed that trust by trying to steal his money."

Edith's accusation struck Eddie hard. That did make him a thief. He should have returned what was left over after new clothes, travel and the cost of food for the journey had been paid. It flattened his sense of righteous indignation.

"Benson is a ghost, isn't he?" Eddie quickly thought of a response to steer the conversation away from the money. He wanted to hang on to it for now, in case it could help him in another escape bid.

"And I looked in the kitchen just now to see objects moving around as if being operated by paranormal forces," he added another distraction.

Edith again responded in a calm, unruffled manner.

"Wait until my husband returns, and all will become clear," she replied, standing up to leave. "Now would you like a meal?"

"No!" Eddie emphatically replied. "I'd like a bottle of whisky and a glass in my room."

"I'll send the butler up with them. Get a good rest tonight, and take the day off tomorrow." Edith gave yet another smile. "I don't want you to feel unwelcome here. The lake is a relaxing place, and there's a rowing boat moored at the jetty. Go for a row. It greatly eases tension." She opened the dining room door and left.

A BOTTLE of whisky and glass were already on the writing desk when Eddie returned to his room.

He'd been considering what Edith had told him. At first he was fleetingly persuaded by her explanation, starting to think it was perfectly rational, and with an opportunity for him in the offing. But it hadn't conveyed anything that explained why he needed to be imprisoned there.

Surely if all was well, the purpose for him being there could have been given at the outset, and presented to him as an opportunity either to accept or decline the offer. Why would Dr Albright not trust his wife to give an accurate description of its nature? She was obviously a perfectly capable person. Eddie concluded neither of them could be trusted.

Right now though, he wanted strong drink and opened the whisky bottle, pouring himself a generous glassful. The warming spirit began to relax him, easing his troubled mind. On an empty stomach its effect rapidly coursed through his body, urging him to pour yet more generous top ups.

Moving from the writing desk chair, he swayed reaching the bed and sitting on it. Now alcohol started to fuzz his mind. Anger began to rise in him at being imprisoned. He got up again, pouring another glass of whisky from the bottle on the desk. He started to stagger as he approached the room door, flinging it open.

"Where are you all, bastards," he slurred down the corridor, his voice echoing into the emptiness. "Are you all bloody ghosts? Benson, I hate you!" All remained eerily silent as his abuse faded away.

Eddie slammed the door shut, totally zapped. Hardly able to keep balance, he staggered to the bed and collapsed on it. Within moments he broke into loud snoring.

THE SUNNY morning didn't greet Eddie joyfully. A thundering headache and dry throat led to a woeful groan as he raised himself from the bed. As he glanced across at the half empty whisky bottle on the table, he gave another groan.

Eddie was unaccustomed to a lot of strong alcohol, and could have been visited by fifty Jeremiahs in the night scraping the chair, without having the slightest notion of noise. But now the knocks on his door felt like hammer blows. He lurched forward to open it. The butler stood stiffly outside.

"Do you require breakfast?" he asked, in his usual monotone.

Eddie had no appetite for food, but thought he ought to try and eat a little of something after not eating for some time. It would either give him sustenance or he'd throw it up. He'd take the chance.

"A boiled egg and a slice of toast, with strong coffee," he groaned again.

Roberts acknowledged the order with a slight nod of the head, and left.

CHAPTER 7

A NEW maid now replaced the unfriendly woman who'd served Eddie. She had greying curls of hair protruding from beneath her white mob cap, and was about the same middle age as the one she followed, though the cheeks were chubbier and she wore an indifferent expression.

"Where's the other maid?" asked Eddie, as she placed the cupped egg, coffee, milk, sugar and toast on the table from a tray. The woman stared blankly at Eddie for a moment, said nothing and left. He raised his eyebrows and quietly mouthed, 'ah well, pleased to meet you too'.

The food and coffee helped to make him feel a little more human again, though the hangover held firmly to his throbbing head.

As he crossed the hall returning to his room, a young man with side-parted fair hair, wearing a short sleeved blue shirt and black trousers, descended the stairway. Eddie wondered who he was, guessing him to be in his early twenties. As they passed Eddie smiled a greeting. The man gave the merest hint of a smile in return, accompanied with a furtive sideways glance before he headed towards a door in the hallway.

Eddie watched him entering the room and closing the door, wondering if the stranger was human or a spectre?

SINCE he'd been given the day off from gardening duties, he decided to take up Edith's suggestion of visiting the lake and going for a row. Maybe it would help clear his mind and still his throbbing head.

As he made his way along the gravel track towards the angel fountain and lake beyond, he saw a number of workers tending to flower beds in the ornamental gardens alongside. It reinforced his conclusion that gardening for a living was not his ambition.

What opportunity was it Edith said her husband had in store for him, in her less than detailed description? Eddie was not convinced it would be to his benefit.

The lake gently rippled in the warm August sunlight, fluffy clouds briefly obscuring the twinkle of the waves. The waters extended across a wide span and length with distant views of surrounding countryside. Ducks began paddling across to him in anticipation that food might be in the offing as he reached the jetty.

Eddie had rowed before on boats along the River Thames at Richmond in Surrey, where he lived some years ago, and was familiar with the activity. Clambering into the boat and wobbling to keep his balance as it rolled in the water, he untied the mooring rope, took the oars and cast off.

Edith was right, the tensions that had strained his mind and body began to ease. The scavenging ducks spread outwards in disappointment for lack of being fed, but also anxious to escape the splashing oars.

As Eddie relaxed, his thoughts began to calmly consider his situation. Suspicion of the possible motives for him being there took centre stage, but more in the sense of a cool headed detective analysis rather than fear. Edith's waffle explanation, his forced detention, and the inexplicable paranormal activity all came in for consideration.

Something extremely odd was obviously being undertaken at the house, and there were apparently ghost entities residing at the property. Benson's ability to disappear and re-appear instantly demonstrated that. The strange man he'd seen by the building with the chimney also gave signs of existing in the other world. The paranormal activity in the kitchen. Was the young man he'd met on the stairs a human or spirit?

All these fragments of information were like jigsaw pieces, that would help towards a rational explanation. But there were missing pieces.

Eddie needed to find more to complete the puzzle. It all needed further research in the house. If he found an opportunity to escape, he could avoid that avenue altogether, which seemed the best option. If he couldn't get away, he definitely had to explore the property further.

After half-an-hour, Eddie reached the far end of the lake, where reeds grew in profusion. Canada geese glided beside and between them. He steered the boat towards the bank just short of the setting. As it touched the shoreline, he glanced up to see Benson standing there staring at him. Eddie felt as if the entity was reading his mind. Thoughts considering a successful break from the place across the fields.

Eddie used an oar to push away from the bank and began rowing away. He glanced back to see if Benson was tracking him along the route, but he'd disappeared. No doubt following unseen, surmised Eddie. There was no likelihood he could escape for now. Getting away was going to be no walkover.

He rowed back to the jetty and returned to the house. He wouldn't attempt any more bank-side landings with thoughts of escape in mind, never knowing for sure whether Benson's watchful eye, visible or invisible, would be cast on him.

Roberts came out of a side door as Eddie crossed the hallway.

"I can bring a light lunch to your room," the man said in his cold, upright manner. With his throbbing head now easing, Eddie's appetite was returning. He made a choice from the offerings the butler recited.

It still struck him as odd, that when he wasn't an ordinary worker on gardening duties, he continued to be treated as an esteemed guest. That is, except when he'd upset Edith by engaging in conversation with Betty about the disused servants' dining quarters.

As he sat at the desk in his room eating lunch from a tray, Eddie resolved to explore the upper floors of the house that night when everything was always eerily quiet. It seemed to him that no-one actually occupied the premises overnight. But occupied or not, he'd also have to risk invisible eyes watching him, though surely even Benson couldn't be everywhere all the time?

That afternoon Eddie entered the landscaped garden, passing workers tending to the flower beds. He'd noticed a side opening in the brick enclosure when he'd been working nearby. A field laid beyond, and he thought it would be good to pass the time with a stroll.

A few hundred yards ahead the field dipped in a steep incline and as he reached it, caught sight of a dilapidated cottage below with a stream on its far side. Curious, Eddie descended the slope and walked towards it.

The tiled roof had mostly caved into the grey stone structure, the chimney stack stood precariously lop-sided, looking like the next candidate ready to collapse. Gaping squares now stared from the property where windows once resided, and the front door was similarly denuded.

Two crows perched on the angled chimney stack, stared suspiciously as Eddie approached. Not waiting to discover if he was friend or foe they took to the air, loudly cawing and soaring across the fields into the distance.

Pieces of stone rubble that had broken from the building were scattered across what might once have been a pretty front garden, bordered now by a decaying low stone wall. Eddie wondered who had lived in such a tranquil setting during the cottage's heyday, with the nearby stream flowing through the meadowland.

"That was the gamekeeper and his wife's home," a man's voice came from behind, as if reading Eddie's thoughts. He turned to see the same bearded man with a flat cap, collar-less shirt, dark red neckerchief and grey trousers, who'd mysteriously appeared beside the locked building during his walk the other day.

"His wife Emma is long gone, God rest her soul. But Rufus still works at the house. They managed to save him when a horse carriage lost a wheel on the Grange's fore-court and toppled on them," the man explained. "The cot-tage has been deserted since then."

Eddie struggled to get a hang on his words, let alone the man's sudden appearance.

The figure drew nearer, smiling as he registered Eddie's bafflement.

"It must have happened a long time ago, you'll be thinking, for the cottage to be in that state," the man said. "And you'll be right. Nearly one hundred years ago, and you'll also be puzzling as to how Rufus could still be working at the house."

Those thoughts had crossed Eddie's mind.

"I'm about the same age as Rufus, but I come from London," the stranger continued. "Just found myself here one day. Understand I was killed when a Hackney cab ran into me when I was crossing the Charing Cross Road with my son. That's what Rufus told me when we worked together here." He paused. "Of course, that's before they chucked me out. Too much trouble for them you see."

Eddie stood transfixed. The man before him had perished at the time of hackney cabs for transport, and Rufus still worked at the house. Both should definitely be dead by now, even if they'd lived to a very old age.

"If you don't want to join Dr Albright's...." The man stopped, as if sensing something. "Benson is looking for you," he said. "Best I go for now. Come down here another time, but don't leave it too long. I'm always around." He disappeared.

Eddie continued to stare transfixed at the spot where the man had been. Everywhere in the place seemed to abound with spectres. And what did the ghost he'd just encountered again mean by 'if you don't want to join Dr Albright's....'

before abruptly stopping. Eddie was roused from his trance seeing Benson descending the slope and approaching.

The spectral estates manager walked by Eddie's side, accompanying him back to the residence. Hardly a word passed between them, other than Benson telling him he was free to roam the grounds, but not to stray too far. The distance Eddie had reached on his walk to the cottage was as far as permitted. The polite manner in which Benson gave the order, contained an underlying threat in its tone if disobeyed.

Back in his room, Eddie decided to take a rest until dinner time, reading his book for a while.

At dinner, he poured a glass of red wine accompanying his meal, the vintage privilege obviously restored. It appeared Edith had got over her annoyance with him for gleaning too much information from the disappeared Betty.

As usual the wine tasted exquisite, but he was determined to keep a clear head for the house search ahead that night, so limited it to one glassful.

The second replacement maid maintained her solemn silence while serving, other than taking his food order, and telling him the lady of the house had granted him another day off work 'on the morrow'.

Eddie again wondered why he was being treated in such an esteemed manner, but was happy to be excused from gardening.

That evening he settled on the bed to read his book, and after a while thought he'd just take a short nap. He woke in a panic, the short nap lasting longer than he'd intended. He shot up, glancing at his watch. It was one fifteen in the morning.

"Thank heaven," he mumbled, realising he still had time to search, and hoping even Benson must now be in some other paranormal place he inhabits. However, it was a thought more in the hope of possibility than likely fact. He'd have to take the chance.

The corridor outside his room was deathly quiet as he carefully opened the door to leave. The dimmed globe lights added to the eerie atmosphere, where in Eddie's heightened state of awareness even a pin dropping might sound like a giveaway peal.

His trainer footsteps seemed to echo along the corridor, even though he trod as lightly as possible. Several times he stopped, thinking he'd heard some other movement, a creak, a footfall. The thumping of his quickening heartbeat now sounded intent on betraying his presence.

Benson had noiselessly appeared when Eddie was in the servants' disused dining room, so now he kept glancing behind, fearing the spectre was about to pounce.

Reaching the first floor landing he surveyed the hall below. Seeing no-one he carefully began ascending the stairway to the second floor. On reaching it, he turned to take the left corridor, creeping along and praying nobody would suddenly open a door and see him. Passing several rooms, he plucked up the courage to try turning the circular brass handle of one, to see if it would open.

It was highly risky should someone be awake inside, but he just had to try. So far in his stay, he'd seen no trace of anyone actually occupying the rooms in the house, save possibly for the young man he'd briefly encountered on the stairs yesterday.

The door was unlocked, and Eddie ever so gently pushed it open, the dim light from the corridor casting a soft sweep of illumination in its path.

He caught sight of a tall object several feet away, which seemed to be covered by a white dust sheet, probably covering a wardrobe, he guessed. More furniture looking to be a chest of drawers, a double bed and dressing table were similarly covered by sheets, indicating the room was unoccupied.

The subdued corridor light was joined by a streak of moonlight shining through the uncurtained window, adding to the silent eeriness of the setting and causing Eddie to give an involuntary shiver. Were ghostly eyes watching him from the shadows?

An urge to return to the relative comfort of his own room came over him, but he resisted in favour of continuing the search.

Since so far he hadn't seemingly been discovered by his ubiquitous warder Benson, Eddie's confidence to carry on was restored a little.

Leaving the room, he crept further along the corridor, cautiously entering more unoccupied ones with dust sheet coverings. He assumed the house in its heyday must have been filled with guests staying in these rooms, probably enjoying field sports weekends and evening soirées with relatives and friends of the family.

This corridor appeared to be fruitless for discovering anything further about the odd activities at Harcourt

Grange, so Eddie decided to try the landing's opposite corridor, though his hope of discovering anything useful was starting to recede.

The first few rooms on the other side yielded nothing more, some of them devoid of any contents. But as he progressed along the route, his ears pricked up at the faint sound of voices. He froze and his heart began pounding again. Was he about to be detected?

His instinct again was to try and get back to his room, but curiosity made him remain still, he wanted to hear what the voices were saying. However, the sound was too far away to make out the words. Keeping his fear under control, he stealthily approached the corridor's end to reach the door where the sounds were coming from.

"Anyway, I'd better get going," came a man's voice. "Larry will be cursing me for not taking over the shift on time. Unit 5 is experiencing some fluid intake problems, and I'm better at controlling the flow than he is."

Eddie heard the turn of the room handle. The door began to open.

"Why Dr Albright chose him to join us here is beyond me," the man continued, opening the door. Another man inside chuckled in agreement at the remark.

Eddie was sloping away, desperately trying to reach the next doorway where he could hide inside undetected. In seconds that seemed like hours, he was able to grip the handle, praying the door was unlocked and unoccupied, but for a moment the door didn't budge. The man was stepping out, glancing back at his companion.

"You go and tell Larry what a hopeless sod he is," the voice inside chuckled.

The sound of the retort was enough for Eddie to shove the door open, hiding a short scrape as he slipped inside, and carefully pushing it almost closed to avoid the sound repeating.

Eddie heard the adjoining door close, and he listened in the room's pitch darkness as the man's footsteps died away along the corridor. Fortunately, he thought, he'd found himself in another unoccupied room. While he waited for a few minutes to be absolutely sure the coast was clear, his eyes began to adjust to the dark, seeing now a little moonlight seepage from the sides of a heavily curtained window.

Suddenly he heard a scuffling sound and froze in terror. It stopped. Eddie's ears were pricked up for all they were worth. Now he could make out shadowy shapes. Again they seemed like furniture covered in dust sheets. Then he glanced at what looked like a double bed. A tiny set of shining eyes greeted him from it. The outline of a small body appeared to be poised on its hind legs, as far as he could tell in the dark.

Eddie remained anchored, as he realised he was staring at a rat. He hated rats. The creatures scared the shit out of him. The rat appeared unphased, continuing to stare at its new room mate. Eddie slowly pulled the door open to leave, determined neither to attract the animal towards him or alert the person remaining in the next room.

Stepping outside, he could hear the sound of a TV coming from the occupied room. It presented a convenient opportunity to cover the scrape as he carefully closed the door and creep back along the landing undiscovered.

As he quietly returned, the words of the man he'd heard leaving the room echoed in his mind, adding to the mystery of the place.

'Larry will be cursing me for not taking over the shift on time. Unit 5 is experiencing some fluid intake problems.'

"What was going on? What was unit 5? Fluid intake problems? Was Dr Albright running some sort of hospital unit here? If so, Eddie thought he might well have seen some medical staff in white gowns. But to date he hadn't.

He got into bed, exhausted with the nervous strain, and wondering if rats might find their way into his room. He lay with questions leaping around in his mind, until he finally slipped into a restless sleep.

"I saw what you were doing," a voice shook him rudely awake. It sounded like the boy Jeremiah in the darkened room.

"Clear off you idiot," Eddie slurred in a half slumber, unable to find the energy to raise himself.

"It's alright, I won't tell anyone," came the youngster's reply. "They treat me like dirt here, and I hate them all. Get out of here if you can."

The comment made Eddie find the strength to raise himself on his elbows. Would this boy be an ally? Filtered moonlight through the curtains seeped into the room, casting outlines of furniture, but nothing else.

"Are you still there Jeremiah? called Eddie.

A form began to materialise at the end of the bed. Soon the figure of a youngster wearing a flat cap, collarless white shirt, brown waistcoat and black trousers appeared.

"Yes, I'm still here," he replied. "Sorry about the tricks of moving and scraping the chair when you arrived. I've got no friends here, and need a bit of fun." The lad sounded genuinely contrite.

Eddie stared at the apparition more in amazement than fear. From his clothing, he looked as if he was from a past era.

"Where do you come from?" Eddie quizzed.

"From London. Lived in a house at Aldgate with my four brothers and three sisters. I was the youngest, and hadn't been expected." Jeremiah replied. "Then not long after I was born me mum got the consumption and died. In the next couple of years, two of me sisters and one of me brothers got the consumption and died. It was hard for dad keeping the rest of us fed and clothed. When the others got jobs, they left home and dad looked after me." The boy seemed keen to tell Eddie his story.

"When did you live there?" asked Eddie, puzzled by his old style clothing.

"Not sure. Me aunt said it was about May or June 1874," he replied. "When I asked mum she always said 'you was a surprise. I never expected you, and I reckon you tired me out'."

Eddie was speechless. If the boy was right on the approximate date of his birth, here definitely was another ghost. His mysterious appearance and moving the chair when disembodied could surely not be the doing of a trickster.

Eddie was about to ask Jeremiah his age, which he guessed was around ten years, and how he came to be at Harcourt Grange, but the youngster suddenly appeared distracted.

"Sorry guv, I've got to go. I can sense there's a trace on me. It's best if I clear off for now. I'll come again though." Jeremiah dissolved.

Propped on his elbows, Eddie rested back and stared upwards into the darkness, trying to fathom what he'd heard and seen. Further sleep seemed impossible, unanswered questions still buzzing in his mind, and wondering if he'd just had a truly realistic dream. Light infrequent dozing was all he could now manage, swiftly awaking from nightmares with loud mocking laughter, and figures in grotesque, distorted bodies lunging at him then disappearing.

CHAPTER 8

AT breakfast next day, Eddie's mind was filled with the previous night's events. His visitation from Jeremiah, and the two men on the second floor.

If only he hadn't needed to hide when one of them came out of the room beside him. Where in the house was he going?

Eddie had the day off, and he wondered how he could fill the hours. Any attempt to explore the house in daylight hours was not an option. Edith, Benson and Roberts the butler were all likely to be around. Last night he got away without being detected by any of them, though obviously the boy had followed him unseen. And he appeared to be a possible ally, not an informant.

Once again it was risky, but Eddie decided he'd try searching again that night. Where next was the only thing he hadn't worked out yet. Returning to the dusty, disused staff dining room that Betty had pointed out to him was a thought. There was another door in the room which he'd been on the point of opening, but Benson had appeared and stopped him before he could enter. Eddie decided to think it over.

He spent the morning strolling around the lawns and fields not far from the house. Then after being served a light lunch by Roberts in his room, Eddie decided to take a look around the exterior of the house to see if there might be any clues to entering it another way, that might lead to this unit 5.

At the back there was a small courtyard set in a central recess of the property. He presumed it might contain tables and chairs for enjoying morning coffee or afternoon tea on warm summer days. At the rear of the recess a railing ran partway across its length. As Eddie approached it he saw a stone stairway inside, leading down to a basement room with a narrow paved path to a side entrance door.

A dusty window overlooked the path. Immediately Eddie recognised it as the window a high moon was shining through when he'd entered the disused servants' dining quarters.

Seeing no-one around he descended the stairs and tried to open the door, hoping it might present an opportunity to enter the door inside he'd been about to open when Benson had appeared. But it was locked.

Returning to the courtyard, Eddie wondered what to do next. He decided to take another stroll to the derelict cottage where he'd encountered the ghost who'd warned him to escape from the house. The spirit had invited him to return there, and who knows, he might be able to help. Eddie remembered his parting words. 'Come another time. I'm always around.'

Eddie crossed the fields and arrived at the ruin, imagining how the cottage would have looked before time and neglect had eroded it. He also wondered if Benson was watching him unseen. This was the marker point he'd been warned not to proceed beyond.

"I thought you'd come again," the voice from behind shook him from his musing. Eddie turned to see the spirit who'd spoken to him at the cottage yesterday.

"I hope my son, Jeremiah, has apologised to you for playing the chair scraping pranks in your room at night," he continued.

"Your son?" Eddie gazed at him in surprise.

"Yes, I'm Franklin his father," the spectre confirmed. "Jeremiah perished by my side when the horse drawn Hanson cab ploughed into us in London," he explained.

Then Franklin's expression turned into a frown. "It was enough that I should end up here, but to condemn my son too, instead of allowing him to meet his maker and rest in peace."

Now the ghost's eyes narrowed in anger. "I hate Dr Albright, and if I can help to save you and destroy that bastard, I'll do all in my power." He paused for a moment, before adding, "I have to say though, my ability to help you is limited. Albright has some powerful forces around him. It won't be easy."

Eddie needed no confirmation on how hard it was likely to be in escaping. But to know he definitely had an ally was comforting. Weird though, he thought. Never in all his days could he have dreamt a ghost would one day be offering to help him. Harcourt Grange certainly was the strangest place.

"Tell me what's happening here?" asked Eddie.

"There's no time to explain now," the spirit replied. "Benson or his watchers will be starting to search for you, to make sure you're not trying to escape. Wait in your room tonight, and when the time is right, my son Jeremiah will visit to tell you more." Franklin disappeared.

Eddie stared at where the ghost had stood, still trying to fathom the bizarre world he had entered at Harcourt Grange.

A short distance ahead in the field, another spectre suddenly materialised. A young, dark haired man, wearing a short-sleeved red check shirt and blue jeans. He approached, staring aggressively at Eddie, as if trying to assess some forbidden motive in his mind.

"I hope you're not planning to go beyond the boundary set for you here," the arrival gave a grim faced warning.

"Who are you?" Eddie asked.

"Doesn't matter who I am. I've just been sent here by Mr Benson to ensure you obey," he replied sharply.

"No, I'm just enjoying a stroll," said Eddie calmly, to give the impression escape could not be further from his mind.

"Good," replied the spirit, and vaporised from sight.

Eddie's already overwhelming sense of hopelessness at Harcourt Grange was crushing enough, and now knowing Benson definitely had other unseen spirits potentially detecting his movements, his hope of ever escaping was depressed even further.

Feeling dejected, he began to make his way back to the house. Gradually the depression was eased a little by growing curiosity of what Jeremiah's visit would bring that night.

CHAPTER 9

EDDIE decided to dispense with the formality of dressing for dinner. He informed Roberts of the decision seeing him in the hall on his return.

"I don't want to eat alone in that God forsaken dining room again. It's about as much fun as seeing your miserable face," he told the butler bluntly.

"As you wish sir," Roberts replied, his dour face registering no emotion at the insult. "I shall serve dinner in your room."

Eddie could have expected that there would be no emotional response from the insult, but it selfishly helped to relieve a little of his frustration.

He was served an excellent salmon meal with vintage wine in his room, but lack of appetite, and a desire not to drift into a deep alcoholic sleep, led him to consume little. He read a book on his bed for a while, growing impatient for Jeremiah's visit. He had no idea when it would be.

Beginning to fight off the urge to sleep, he occasionally paced the room. At twelve thirty in the morning, he began to doubt the spirit boy would arrive, but decided to give it just a little longer before going to bed.

Just at the point of giving up, Jeremiah materialised by the wardrobe.

"Sorry I'm so late," he started with a cheeky grin, "but I had to make sure that bastard Benson had finished snooping round the house," he explained. "I can evade him and his watchdogs pretty easy, but they can throw me out if they catch me." He shook his head while maintaining the grin.

"And you've got a real body that's got no chance of disappearing quick if anyone's on to us," he added, "so I have to be extra careful." Jeremiah disappeared from his position beside the wardrobe, re-appearing a second later by the room door.

"See, I can move like that, but I'll have to remain visible so you can follow me."

"Follow you? Can you tell me what's going on here?" Eddie was growing increasingly frustrated in the delay to find out what was happening in the house.

"I'm going to take you to the basement room where Dr Albright keeps his secrets," the spirit told him.

"What secrets?" Now Eddie grew ever more desperate to find out what was going on.

"Ssh!" the boy put his finger to his lips as he opened the door. "Come on," he whispered, beckoning him to follow.

Eddie obeyed, treading as lightly as he could in his trainers along the corridor, while Jeremiah's black hobnail boots made no sound as they touched the floor.

The boy reached the landing, then opened the first door on the right in the opposite corridor. It was one Eddie hadn't tried on his previous sortie.

The low level lighting continued as the spirit entered with his mystified companion behind. A short corridor ahead led to a wooden stairway. They descended, passing a small landing with a double sided corridor. At the bottom of the flight they approached a door.

"Now I'm going to disappear," the spirit whispered. "Give me a few seconds so I can cause a distraction inside, then open the door and come in."

Eddie nodded agreement.

"But just take a quick look though, no more than 30 seconds. Best if you're not seen in there." Jeremiah vaporised from view.

Eddie waited a few seconds, then opened the door.

He squinted for a moment as his eyes met a brightly illuminated room. Swiftly adjusting, they met the sight of a wide long room, the white walls lending a sanitised atmosphere.

Inside, Jeremiah was jumping up and down, making silly rasping noises and distracting a young man seated at a monitor on a long shelf, that also supported a row of other monitors with facing seating. The man rose to tackle him.

"Get out of here!" he shouted at the boy, his back turned to the Eddie, who'd caught sight of a long row of glass tanks supported on a sturdy wooden base the other side of the room.

In a cursory glance, Eddie thought they were fish tanks. Then he reeled back in shock, realising there was no aquatic life inside them. They contained human brains, suspended in a light brown liquid.

The horrific display chilled his blood, but he couldn't resist approaching the sight and lingering out of spellbound curiosity.

Jeremiah's noise and cavorting were driving the young man to distraction as he attempted to tackle him, but he was powerless to seize a spirit that could be solid for one second, then become invisible and untouchable the next.

He turned and pressed an alarm pad on the shelf, now catching sight of Eddie, who'd overstayed the time Jeremiah had advised.

"What are you doing here? Get out!" the man yelled at him. It broke Eddie's trance and he rapidly turned to leave, only to be confronted by Benson.

"You really are taking a lot of liberties," the sullen estate manager growled aggressively. "Now do as you're told and leave. If I discover you are entering territory uninvited again, or attempting some stupid escape, I'll ensure you are locked in a secure room for 24 hours a day, and given food fit only for an animal."

Eddie shuffled out of the room, annoyed with himself for being discovered by remaining too long when he'd been told only to take a brief look and leave.

"It's that bloody Jeremiah kid," Eddie heard the young man explaining to Benson, as he began closing the door behind him. "He's disappeared now, but if only we could find a way of keeping him out."

Eddie closed the door and began returning to his room, the sight of human brains in tanks searingly etched in his mind.

What the hell is going on here? He knew that Albright was a surgeon, and now he began to wonder if he was a brain specialist. But why would he have them displayed in a grisly parade in his own home?

Bringing home the brains of deceased patients for research was something that might have happened in the long past. Surely though, not a practise allowed in the 21st century? No wonder the surgeon wanted to keep it secret.

As he entered his room and closed the door, a terrifying thought came to him. Was that why he was being held prisoner, and effectively being kept a secret himself from the outside world? Did the surgeon want to do research on Eddie's brain, wired up so Albright could examine brainwave patterns on the monitor screens in the basement?

But those brains were in tanks of fluid. They had no bodies. Now Eddie began to shake with fear. Surely not? No, the surgeon couldn't do that, surely?

He began to think perhaps he could. No one in the outside world was likely to miss him. Set up an alarm. And if so, it was unlikely to be for a very long time. He'd been disowned by Steph his ex-partner, and no-one else knew where he might be.

Eddie sat on the bed in a confused state, wanting to cut out such macabre thoughts, but they insisted on coming to the fore.

Would Jeremiah shortly re-appear and explain what it was all about, hopefully reassuring him the fate he now started to fear was just a ridiculous notion? Time passed, and Jeremiah did not re-appear.

EDDIE wasn't sure if he'd actually slept that night, or had slumped into a merciful, trouble free coma. Morning light greeted his flickering eyes as they opened. He didn't remember laying down on the bed, but now stared from it at the ceiling.

Instantly he sprang up as thoughts of the previous night struck him. He had to escape from this hell hole. Find a way through the security. Though how? Everywhere he went was spied on.

Eating breakfast was certainly not on his agenda. He'd drop into the dining room for a coffee to stimulate his mind. In the hallway he met Roberts coming from a doorway and approaching to speak.

"Sod off stiff shirt," Eddie shouted angrily at him, delivering fury at this facade of respectability that hid the gruesome undercurrent of Harcourt Grange.

"As you wish, sir," the butler replied, again no hint of emotion showing in his granite demeanor, and returned back to the room he'd just left.

Feeling a little refreshed after his coffee, Eddie decided to go for a walk and attempt to clear his head. Perhaps come up with an escape plan. Edith and Mulch hadn't instructed him to do anything, so he took it he wasn't needed.

He decided to stroll down to the building on the other side of the stream where he'd first encountered the spectre Franklin. As he crossed the bridge, he stopped halfway to absorb the leafy, peaceful setting all around. For a few moments, chirruping birds and crayfish darting in the clear rippling water beneath, had the effect of soothing his mind a little.

"You should have got out of there quicker," a boy's voice wrenched Eddie from his calmer thoughts. He looked to see Jeremiah standing on the other side.

"I couldn't believe what I was seeing," Eddie replied defensively.

"Nah, and most wouldn't," the boy agreed. "Now follow me. I've checked and Benson and his crew ain't out looking for you yet."

Jeremiah led him to the building with the chimney tube and high frosted windows. As they reached it, Franklin suddenly appeared out of the air.

"My son here," the spirit indicated Jeremiah beside him, "tells me you ran into trouble last night."

Eddie nodded.

"Horrible sight, eh? Brains in tanks, like a bloody display of human trophies," Franklin shook his head in disgust.

"Well they ain't got mine or my son's stuck in there anymore, and that causes them a big problem," the spectre smiled.

"Why would they be there?" Eddie enquired earnestly.

"Tell you in a minute. But first you've been wondering why this building is here," Franklin pointed at the structure. Eddie nodded again.

"It's Albright's private crematorium," the spirit announced, sending another revelation shock wave through Eddie.

"He removes people's brains and burns the rest of their bodies in there." Franklin could see the information left a look of horror on Eddie.

"Of course," the spirit continued, "all the older ones, like me and my son, had our brains removed many long years ago, just after we'd died, by a surgeon at a London hospital who preserved them by a special process."

Father and son glanced at each other as if sensing something. Then Jeremiah disappeared.

"The more recent brains in his collection," Franklin went on, "were from people who came to the Grange not realising Albright was planning to remove them, and dispose of their bodies...whoosh!" He motioned towards the cremation building.

The full terror of what awaited Eddie came home. His brain was going to join the surgeon's collection.

"But what's it for?" Eddie was confounded. "Research?"

"Oh, more than that," Franklin replied.

Jeremiah now reappeared.

"One of Benson's lot is coming," he warned. Father and son instantly disappeared.

Eddie was desperate to discover why Albright was removing people's brains. But the moment was gone. Though even if he knew, it would be no consolation as to his fate.

Within seconds a man who looked to be in his thirties appeared from nowhere facing Eddie. He wore a grey shirt with rolled up sleeves, revealing muscular arms, and dark red trousers. His flat nose, and face scarred with lines that seemed like knife slashes, appeared fearful enough, without the menacing eyes staring at him.

"Time for walkies back to the house," he snarled, and dissolved from view. Eddie took the obligatory hint.

Albright's refuge ploy to invite him to Harcourt Grange was now revealed. The surgeon wanted to extract his brain, and burn his body in that private cremation furnace.

It was such a hideous notion, that his mind began producing its own tranquiliser to prevent him from cracking up on the spot.

He walked back to the house in a trance, the inability to conceive a way of escape draining him in the manner of a prisoner condemned to an imminent death sentence.

The light gardening duties, the sumptuous meals and wines, butler service, being given the best, now added up to pleasantries to be enjoyed before the sentence was carried out, Eddie realised.

"Enjoy your walk?" Edith's voice pulled him from his troubled reverie. Eddie was approaching the front entrance of the house as she was coming down the steps.

He gazed at her in disgust. Her greeting face fell, seeming puzzled by his reaction.

"Don't try and pretend you don't know what's going on," he growled. "You've been stringing me along, knowing all the time I'm here to be killed, have my brain taken out, and probably used for some experiment by the low life murderer you call a husband."

"Who have you been talking to?" the woman demanded. "Is it Franklin or Jeremiah?"

Eddie said nothing.

"It is, isn't it?" she said sharply. Eddie continued to say nothing.

"They're nothing but trouble," she spoke more for her own musing than Eddie's benefit.

"Well they're right aren't they?" said Eddie. Edith stared at him confused, unable to deny it was true.

"If I'm not here to be used as some sort of guinea pig for experiment, then release me from this place so I can go on my way," Eddie challenged.

Edith gazed at him as if he'd just called checkmate in the clash, then stormed off.

His surge of fury had the effect of lifting him from his depressed stupor. The will to overcome these despots sparked into life. How he was going to achieve it, however, still eluded him. But now confidence pushed aside doubt.

Although now living with the knowledge he was a condemned man, unlike other revelations that had dimmed his appetite, he was feeling hungry that evening.

He entered the dining room to be met by the joyless maid, and he wondered whether she'd ever been able to ever raise a smile. Her personality, or lack of, would make a perfect match with Roberts the butler, he thought.

"The lady of the house, Mrs Albright, says you can have ham or cheese sandwiches for dinner. Eddie realised this drop in choice of evening meal was Edith's revenge for daring to challenge her.

"Can I have ham and cheese in a sandwich, or even cheese and ham in a sandwich together?" Eddie posed, seeing a momentary puzzled expression, as if she was trying to work out whether there was any difference in the combination.

Her sour face filled with fury, realising Eddie was taking the piss.

"And a cup of coffee," he said, knowing wine would not be on offer tonight. The maid left for the kitchen.

Afterwards Eddie returned to his room and rested on the bed, considering possibilities for escape, the uppermost method perhaps by finding a way to distract his watchers long enough to clear the area.

At around nine o'clock there was a knock on the door. Could it be Jeremiah? Unlikely, since he didn't bother about barriers. Eddie opened it to see the butler.

"Mrs Albright has asked me to inform you that Dr Albright will be arriving at the house tomorrow morning at ten o'clock, and wishes to seek an audience with you in the sitting room," he delivered the message in his usual dour manner.

"You mean he wants to see me in the sitting room at ten tomorrow," Eddie rephrased, cutting through Roberts' formal old fashioned gobbledegook. The messenger remained expressionless and left.

Eddie wondered what the surgeon had in mind for the meeting. He didn't feel he could greet the man in grateful thanks for offering him a refuge. On the other hand he intended to keep his cool, in the hope that anything the doctor said might give him a clue to escaping from the place. Just having a clash with him from the outset could result in being locked up in a room until the dreaded moment.

He'd wondered regretfully afterwards if his strong words with Edith might result in a stricter punishment of confinement. Fortunately, a meagre dinner was not a severe penalty.

Then a surge of fear struck. Did the surgeon plan to remove his brain tomorrow? Another uneasy night's sleep followed.

CHAPTER 10

EDDIE entered the sitting room at ten next morning.

"Good to see you again," Dr Albright was seated on an ochre sofa, beside him another man. On the small table in front rested a top hat.

The surgeon rose to shake Eddie's hand, looking immaculately dressed in his dark suit, white shirt and royal blue tie.

"This is Thaddeus Albright" the surgeon announced, indicating the man on the sofa, who now rose to greet him. Eddie was taken aback for a moment, casting eyes over him. The elderly gent raised a formal smile between his silvery beard, matching his thinning combed-back hair.

He wore a black frock coat over a white dress shirt, with Waldorf collar and cream cravat tie. Grey trousers and black patent leather shoes completed his clothing. This was the dress of some well to do man of the past, maybe 19th century thought Eddie, staring in curiosity.

"Ah, you're wondering about Thaddeus' attire," said the surgeon. "He is my great, great, great grandfather," he announced, taking relish at Eddie's stunned reaction. He was no quick calculator as to how far back in years that must amount to, but with Albright being at least fifty, the man beside him must have been alive in the mid to late 1800s. Without doubt he'd be dead by now.

The old gent now widened the smile that had first greeted Eddie, stretching the wrinkle lines around his eyes.

"How can he be your, great, great, great grandfather?" asked Eddie. The house was steeped in weirdness, but this was a new dimension of weird.

"Now that is why I've called this little meeting," Albright the younger replied. "I'm going to show you probably the most amazing event that has been achieved by mankind, but for ethical reasons I daren't reveal to the world as yet."

Whatever Eddie had expected from this meet, it certainly wasn't an announcement like that.

"I hear you've already had a brief glance at the wonders in our basement, and now I want to explain to you exactly what it's about," said the surgeon, moving towards the door, followed by his ancient relative and Eddie.

They entered the hall and made their way to the door under the stairway.

"Very remiss that this door wasn't locked the night you trespassed in here, after hearing Betty's tittle tattle about the servants' dining room," said Dr Albright, opening the door.

"That room hasn't been used for years, and we certainly don't need servant dining quarters these days." The surgeon turned, exchanging mischievous smiles between him and his several generations removed granddad, who carried his top hat tucked under his left arm.

They walked along the corridor Eddie had first taken by himself the other night, but this time turning to the right, in the opposite direction to the abandoned dining room. This route linked to the one Jeremiah had shown him.

Down the stairway, they reached the door opening into the chamber of horrors, as Eddie now recalled the event, his heart starting to pump hard.

The shock was no less powerful either, seeing the long line-up of human brains in tanks on one side of the clinical white walled setting.

"Beautiful, isn't it?" said Albright junior, giving a sweep with his arm at the vista.

"Horrific!" retorted Eddie, cringing in disgust.

"Oh, do you think so?" the surgeon sounded a little disappointed. "But then you don't know the miracle of medical science they represent," Albright added proudly. He turned to a young woman on the other side of the room, sitting at one of the monitors on the long shelf. "Don't you think they're beautiful Jodie?"

She swung round on her swivel chair.

"An absolute marvel," she responded, standing up. Her eyes gleamed through her blue framed spectacles, as she brushed back the chestnut brown hair fringe slightly obscuring the right frame. Jodie's demeanour almost glowed, seeming to acknowledge she was being addressed by a great man.

"There you are, someone agrees with me," said the surgeon, turning back to Eddie with a smile, while the woman resumed her seat at the monitor.

"Who did these brains belong to?" Eddie asked, curiosity aroused despite his repulsion at the scene.

"You've seen many of the owners all over the estate and house," the surgeon enlightened him, slowly moving along the line and studying the twists and curves of the spongy globular shapes inside the glass tanks, Eddie and Thaddeus following. The doctor stopped at one of the specimens.

"This is yours, isn't it Thaddeus?" he nodded towards the tank, then turned to his aged relative.

"Indeed, it is?" he replied in a deep voice, "and in as good a condition as the day it was removed from my skull."

Eddie's jaw dropped as he stared at the man. No, not a man, a ghost. But a ghost split between the dead and the living. What unholy creation was this?

"So these are the brains of all the so called people I've seen in this place?" Eddie sought confirmation.

"Well, not all of them," the surgeon answered. "You are all flesh and blood, aren't you Jodie?" he called across to her at the monitor.

She turned and nodded.

"I am too, as are some others you've seen," Albright told him.

Eddie wondered how long he would be remaining in the ranks of the living.

"This all represents generations of experience in my family," the surgeon continued boastfully.

"It certainly does," Thaddeus endorsed the boast. "Yes, it was me that developed a process that could restore and preserve brain functions in a chemical fluid for an indefinite period, if they hadn't been too damaged," he took up the story.

"I was a brain surgeon and came up with the formula in 1887 when I was forty, working in a London hospital." He took the the top hat from under his arm and clasped it between his hands, head slightly tilted recalling the past.

"I'd experimented on many people's brains who had perished in accidents, so that studies could be made before they deteriorated too quickly. Preservation was the problem, so I developed the solution so the brain could be removed and the body disposed. It helped me to carry out useful research that may otherwise have been lost." He paused, reflecting on the memory of his younger living days.

"My son followed in my medical steps, and at my request removed my brain on my death, preserving it in the fluid. It was the early days of electrical discoveries, and before I died we wondered if there might be a possibility of revitalising, even communicating with brains, using an electric current."

Thaddeus stopped again, looking at his brain in the tank, knowing exactly which region of it this memory was coming from.

"There had been experiments around this time using early, crude electrical apparatus to try and revive dead bodies," he continued, turning to Eddie, "but the technology just wasn't developed for tackling the possibility. So we set up this room in the basement for storing brains, in the hope that a way could eventually be found." Thaddeus looked around the room. "Of course, it had none of the equipment now installed here."

"Subsequent sons in the family followed in brain surgery careers," Albright the younger took up the story. "Unfortunately due to circumstances, they were unable to preserve successfully older members of our family, either because brain removal went wrong, dementia had set in, or they were travelling and too far from facilities to extract the brain before rot set in."

He glanced at his bygone relative. "Thaddeus' brain was the only one to make it through."

Eddie remained speechless all this time. His mind was trying to fathom the strangeness of the narrative, which in other circumstances could be dismissed as an absurd fiction. But in front of him was the long line of brains in tanks, in addition to the weird experiences he'd encountered at the house.

"Of course, in earlier times surgeons, and medical men were held in the highest esteem, almost godlike," younger Albright broke in. "Body parts could be removed from hospitals for studies and experiments in surgeons' own private quarters. And if there was a shortage, some of the more unscrupulous surgeons bought bodies from murder victims."

The older surgeon gave an almost imperceptible nod, as if acknowledging that at some time he'd been party to an act of killing like this for studies.

"Nowadays," Albright junior rested back on a small gap between two tanks on the support shelf, "there are so many regulations, it's impossible to remove body parts from hospitals without official forms and approvals. Even then, studies have to be done under the strictest observation." He shook his head disapprovingly.

"So," he straightened again, "our collection here is made up mainly from brains of past generations, collected and preserved when there was no strict official administration. A smaller number are from people in more recent times, kindly donating their brains privately to me for medical science," the surgeon gave a sly smile.

His last words filled Eddie with horror. It was a cynical euphemism for murder, and largely confirmed the fate that lay in store for him.

"You haven't told our friend about the brilliance of your wife Edith," the old Albright prompted.

"Ah yes, Edith," the surgeon began walking towards a door at the end of the grisly tanks line, then stopped. "You see the cables and tubes entering the top of the tanks," he pointed. Eddie hadn't noticed them on his first visit, events had moved too fast. But now he had, and was curious to know their purpose.

"The translucent tubes with the light brown fluid keeps constant renewal of the preserving chemical. The thick grey cables next to them provide waterproof wiring connections into the brains," Albright explained. "The monitoring of them is controlled over there," the surgeon indicated the young woman, Jodie, presently studying her screen.

"But the brilliance of it all was developed by my wife," he added, his eyes gleaming. He continued to the door and began reaching for the handle, then stopped again to face Eddie.

"We met ten years ago at the hospital where I work. The town where you had your catering business," Albright recounted. "She joined to develop our IT division. Her knowledge of computing software is amazing. She solved many problems for us."

"A brilliant woman indeed," Thaddeus added his compliment.

"We worked closely on a project and grew attached to each other, later getting married," the surgeon continued. "When I'd first brought Edith here, she'd marvelled at the brain collection..." he was interrupted by a young man entering the room.

Eddie quickly recognised him as the person who'd ordered him out of the centre the night Jeremiah had brought him here.

"We've had a report Franklin and his son have been getting too close to the house," The man told Albright, as he made his way to a monitor beside Jodie and turned it on.

"Those bloody two," the surgeon's face reddened with anger. "There must be some way we can confine them." He crossed to get a view of what was happening, followed by Thaddeus and Eddie.

"I'm tracking them now," the young man's voice grew animated gazing at the screen as if on the scent of a hunt. Eddie thought it had the imagery of an air traffic controller's monitor, different numbered dots spread around.

"Yes, I've contacted Benson, and now his crew is moving on them. They're retreating back into the estate," the young assistant declared triumphantly after a few minutes.

"I thought I'd disposed of those two spirits long ago," Albright grumbled to Thaddeus. "That kid Jeremiah seems able to find his way into this house a lot of times without us being able to track him."

"A vagabond boy," Thaddeus gave his opinion. "I expect he was able to find his way unnoticed into houses and steal property when he was alive," he condemned the youngster, considering him typical of the lower classes.

"Where was I?" Albright's eyes squinted, trying to recall the direction of his conversation.

"You'd been telling me about the old days when medical men could just take body parts from hospitals without permission," Eddie reminded, sarcastically voicing his disapproval, and looking pointedly at Thaddeus, as if to say it wasn't only the lower classes capable of taking things without consent.

"Then you were saying how brilliant your wife is."

"Ah yes," Albright continued, taking up the thread and crossing back to the door he'd been about to open before the interruption. "When Edith arrived, the brains were just suspended in the preservation fluid. She suggested it might be worth trying to create a system whereby we might be able to communicate with them. It was an idea that had been the target for generations back, but lacking the technology."

He opened the door and light came on illuminating a waist high, grey metal cabinet with ventilation slits along its ten feet length.

"This is the back-up generator room," Albright explained. "It's imperative we don't lose electrical power should the main grid supply cut out."

He hoisted himself to sit on the surface of the presently dormant machinery, explaining that his back often ached from an injury he'd suffered a few years earlier.

"Edith had the idea that if we could connect the brains to an electricity supply, we might be able through a computer to tap into the knowledge stored in them, since electricity powers our minds," he told Eddie. The physician arched his back to try and relieve the ache.

"It also meant setting up cabling for which we employed two electricians, giving them board here. That meant, of course, having to eliminate them when the work was finished. We couldn't rely on them keeping the work secret." The surgeon delivered the words of their fate coldly, no sense of regret in his tone.

Eddie surmised they'd probably been disposed in the surgeon's home fashioned cremation furnace, and their ashes disposed in the grounds. Probably the same fate everyone else had suffered who he'd lured to murder at the house for their brains.

A shiver ran through Eddie, knowing it would be his own fate if he didn't find a way to escape. Even now he wondered if it was too late. That Albright may have planned to carry out his dark work that day. The surgeon didn't appear to notice the pale complexion growing on Eddie's face, as his blood drained in fear at the thought. The surgeon proudly continued his tale as Thaddeus still grasping his top hat decided to replace it on his head.

"Our first breakthrough, a few years later, came when we were able to communicate with the brain of the person you know as Mulch, using the computer to convert his brainwave patterns into speech," the surgeon gazed at Eddie.

"Two more years of experiments then led us to the most incredible device yet," excitement at the memory registered in Albright's voice and gleaming eyes.

He slid off the generator, and began approaching another door. Once again a light came on as they entered, revealing a long room with another row of monitors to one side.

At the far end stood a tall, open fronted cabinet about three feet wide. The side panels were battleship grey and a metallic, silver conical hood stretched above the enclosure, with a thick cable rising from its point into the ceiling. A shiny steel platform covered the base.

Eddie stared at the apparatus, completely baffled by the sight.

"We call this the rebirthing room," Albright announced, bristling with pride. "And all thanks to my genius wife, Edith."

"Here, here," Thaddeus chimed. "Never thought a woman could be capable of creating such wonders back in my day," he added patronisingly.

As he spoke, the woman he'd patronised entered the room.

"Stay," said Edith. "We have a new rebirthing about to happen, I'm sure you'd like to see it," she addressed Eddie, her enthusiastic invitation doubling as an order.

"Can you give me a moment?" Albright asked his wife.

"Yes, I'll wait until you're ready."

"Over there, is the ultimate breakthrough," he continued for Eddie's benefit, pointing to the coned apparatus. "After two more years of experiments, Edith and I discovered how to materialise bodies from the 19th century brain owners after successfully creating that device. And now you can see what I mean."

"Right, go ahead now," said Albright. "I presume our new recruit is the one whose brain I removed a couple of weeks ago?"

Edith nodded.

"You'll have to put on eye protection to prevent yourself from being blinded," she told Eddie, approaching a small cabinet nearby, and taking out protective glasses for them to wear. Thaddeus didn't need them, having no bodily tissues to damage. The ultra light blocking lenses left Eddie hardly able to see anything at all.

Edith lifted a transceiver resting on the top of the cabinet and spoke into it, giving the start command to the control room.

An intensely bright light flashed from the coned hood over the cabinet, lasting for several seconds, then extinguished.

"You can take off the glasses now," said Edith.

As Eddie removed his, he could see the figure of a naked young man now standing inside the apparatus. He was staring around, looking bewildered. Clothing began to appear on him, a light blue T-shirt, black jeans and red trainers.

"That's the control room generating clothing," explained Albright. "We like to dress new recruits in the clothes they were wearing just before their demise. Makes them feel more at home. Of course, we can generate clothing of any kind, but usually stick to the fashion of their own era."

Edith was now approaching the new incarnation, taking his arm to lead him from the device and out of the room.

"They're usually confused at first," Albright continued addressing Eddie as if he was a student. "But Edith is very good with them, helping newcomers acclimatise to their new spirit status. Takes a little time to re-adjust in matters of moving, handling things, disappearing and re-appearing. But you'll soon adapt to it."

Albright now looked at Eddie, whose mouth was wide open at what he'd witnessed.

"Don't worry," he assured with a smile, "it is a quite painless procedure. I'm skilled at minimising the distress of an operation. And Edith will be on hand when you materialise."

The assurance did not assure Eddie. He felt his legs trembling again at the thought of being murdered in cold blood, then next appearing as a spirit in that ungodly device.

Albright began approaching another door to the side of the room, then stopped with his hand resting on the handle.

"In here is my operating theatre," he explained, beginning to open the door. He stopped again. "But of course, there's nothing particularly inventive in there. I'm sure you know what an operating theatre looks like." He pulled the door shut, but not before Eddie had glimpsed some operating tools on a trolley inside, a hand held power saw, chisels, hooks, scalpels and needles.

He visualised the power saw being used to slice off the top of his head, and had to fight hard to overcome the intense feeling of throwing up.

"Come let's return," said Albright, brushing past Eddie, and heading back to the control centre, where the young man and woman still sat at their monitors.

"The beauty of the system is we can program our new-borns not to go beyond the confines of the grounds, except of course for Thaddeus and our trusted servant Benson," continued the surgeon, reaching the control room exit.

Eddie wasn't in the mood to hear any more of Albright's boasting. All he wanted was to escape as quickly as possible. The three of them now approached the stairs outside the control centre.

"Where possible, we generally set our spirits tasks that were their stock in trade when they were alive, using the skills stored in their brains," Albright carried on proudly. "Take Benson, one of our later additions. I invited him here when he was down and out, and sitting on a bench in the park where I met you." They now reached the top of the stairs.

"He'd been the area manager of a major hotel chain and had good organisational skills," the surgeon continued. "Unfortunately he attacked one of the top directors of the chain in a heated argument and, of course, soon found himself out of a job. Unable to get another high level one, he gradually went downhill and became friendless. Now he's a great asset to us."

They approached the door leading back into the hall.

"Another asset," Albright smiled smugly, "is we don't have to provide food for spirits. And those ones not required for current duties, we can temporarily shut down."

Eddie was stunned by the fact that Albright was boasting about these accomplishments and benefits, as if he was trying to impress a visitor or buyer of a service, instead of obliquely informing him that soon he'd be part of this ungodly conception.

Back in the hall, Albright and Thaddeus prepared to depart. The aged spirit patted Eddie on the shoulder.

"I'm sure you'll make an excellent servant here," Thaddeus said to Eddie, "and I believe he has a position of responsibility in mind for you."

"Yes, I think he'll make a good manager of the kitchen staff," the surgeon confirmed. "He has experience of catering."

Eddie felt intimidated by the patronising comment, but realised if Albright took control of his brain and spirit body, he'd have little option but to obey.

"Right, I must be off," said Thaddeus, instantly disappearing into the ether.

"He has a flat in London that I rent for him," explained the surgeon. "He can enjoy many things just as he did in life. The only shortcoming is not being able to taste food or drink," he paused. "But Edith and I are working on a project of brain stimulation that will produce these sensations for our staff. Give them a little perk," he added smugly.

"Now I have an appointment at the hospital," Albright snapped back to the everyday. "I shall return in a day or so, then we can get down to the business," he glanced at Eddie with a grin, delivering his words as if he was arranging a meeting to discuss work matters with a colleague, rather an intention to commit murder.

Eddie stared after him, speechless and stunned as the surgeon made his way to the front door. Unless he could find a way out of this hell very soon, his existence would be far worse than complete death. He remained transfixed, watching the surgeon cross the hall and exit.

CHAPTER 11

EDDIE returned to his room to rest and settle his nerves for a while, as well as be near a toilet with his system remaining on the verge vomiting.

The bizarre tour he'd just endured kept replaying in his mind. He couldn't deny it was all the work of pure genius, but rooted in a total corruption of the natural order.

It was right to try and preserve a person's life if possible, so they could continue living. But to hijack the process between life and death to enslave their spirits and exploit them as servants was pure evil. And soon he would be killed for the same purpose. Another half ghost between the living and the dead.

An hour later, feeling as restored as it was possible in the given circumstances of his perilous future, he decided to go outside for fresh air.

"I hope you found my husband's guided tour interesting," Edith's voice shook Eddie from his thoughts, approaching him on the stairway as he stood outside the front door. He acknowledged her with a cold stare. She stopped a few feet from him.

"Are you looking for words of praise about your genius," Eddie remained aloof. Edith's eyes darted, trying to calculate what he was driving at, and stuck for an immediate reply.

"It's a pity you didn't use your intelligence to create something that would benefit people, instead of murdering them and turning them into slaves," Eddie delivered coldly.

He walked past her and descended the steps, heading along the path towards the fountain, wondering if his words had hit home, or if she was just a psychopath with no feeling for the suffering of others. Edith stared after him for a moment, then entered the house.

A short way along, Eddie left the path leading on to the fountain and decided to head for the derelict cottage. It was a pleasant walk across the fields, and would give him a quiet moment to try and come up with an escape plan. Opportunity was closing fast, and being potentially under surveillance by spirits at any time left him with little if any options.

He reached the cottage ruins. Seeing them made him consider how his own life lay in a ruin. The ambitions he'd harboured not so long ago to succeed in business, be happy and wealthy.

"I got in there for a while when Albright took you on his tour," a young voice came from Eddie's left side. "Managed to slip in there undetected after they thought they'd driven me and dad away from the place." It sounded like Jeremiah. Eddie turned to look, but the lad wasn't visible. Then in a flash he appeared.

"My son is a right slippery one," a man's voice came from Eddie's other side. He turned to see Franklin grinning.

"There has to be a way to get you out of this place," said Jeremiah. "Albright has to be stopped. He's got away with killing too many people for his horrible experiments." He paused. "Well worse really. Leaving them half dead."

The welcoming grin for Eddie now fell from Franklin's face as he grunted agreement with his son.

"Right now escape seems a complete impossibility for me," Eddie shook his head. "I've racked my brain, but there are eyes on me practically all the time."

"If you can think of a way, we'd be only too happy to help," Franklin offered. "We've tried to help people he's lured here before, but he's operated on them almost straight away. You're probably the longest time he's left it before cutting them up."

Eddie winced at the graphic last remark.

"They can't control me and dad or make us do their bidding. Though they can force us back if we get too close or inside the house," explained Jeremiah. "But as you know I can slip in there for a while now and again. And as dad said, if you can think of a way to get out, we'll do our best to help."

"How come they can control the other spirits, but not you?" asked Eddie.

"We were trouble for Albright from the outset," Franklin explained. "The surgeon and his wife had our brains wired up just like the others, but there was always a streak of defiance in me and Jeremiah against authority. Probably part of our brain make-up." He chuckled as he recalled the memory, while Eddie settled on an intact section of the cottage's crumbling front garden wall.

"God knows we had to survive by our wits in the run-down parts of London where we lived. I had a business as a chimney sweep," the spirit nodded towards his son. "And Jeremiah being small enough, used to climb up the chimneys to sweep the soot out with a brush." Franklin's expression grew serious. "Killing you though wasn't it son?" Jeremiah's grim expression was answer enough. "Soot filling his lungs. He couldn't stop coughing. I'd have to find another trade."

"Then me wife caught the consumption," he continued, "and died from it a few months later, God rest her soul. Everything felt pointless after that, so me and the boy decided to go on the road. Sold all the chimney sweep equipment, left our lodgings and bought a stall so we could sell fruit and vegetables in Spitalfields market," Franklin paused, reflecting on the occasion.

Jeremiah glided to a section of the intact garden wall near Eddie to sit beside him. The spirit had no need to rest, but he'd grown fond of Eddie, sensing he was a kind person. Eddie gave him a sympathetic glance, gaining more understanding of what the boy must have suffered in his early years.

"Trouble was," continued Franklin, "we were new to the game. The experienced traders resented us as rivals, and got the fruit and vegetable suppliers, who they knew well, to mark up the better goods at a much higher price when selling them to us. So we could only afford poor quality goods," Franklin grimaced, "and, of course, not many wanted to buy them. Soon we ran out of money." He lowered his head, feeling shame at his lack of success.

"We ended up living on derelict sites among the tramps and winos, scrounging food, taking it out of bins, our clothes dirty. No-one wanted to give me a job looking like I did."

"Then we struck lucky," Jeremiah broke in.

"We did son," his father agreed. "A charity worker came one night when we were settling down in an old building. Gave us some money to clean up, get some new clothes and food. Then helped us get jobs as porters at King's Cross railway station."

"Didn't last too long though," Jeremiah piped in again.

"No, unfortunately not," Franklin agreed. "Not long after we were both run down by a hackney cab on the way back to our lodgings, and knew nothing else until Albright and his wife revived us here." He shook his head. "Took us a bit of time to realise we were all but dead, apart from our brains."

"They've gone now too," said the boy.

"They have son," confirmed his father.

"Then how come you're still here?" Eddie was puzzled.

"No idea," Franklin replied. "Seems we're fully fledged ghosts."

Eddie thought that was the most bizarre statement he'd ever heard. It sounded like there was some form of grading to become a proper ghost. He slid off the garden wall, arching his back to ease stiffness.

"All we know is Albright decided to get rid of us," Franklin continued his explanation. "As I said we was always trouble. For some reason his modern machinery, don't ask me how it all works, couldn't totally control us. We could quite often disobey orders, and him and his wife couldn't do anything about it. So they shut us down, and burnt our brains in that cremation building, near where we first met up. That didn't get rid of us either."

"Wouldn't you rather have found eternal rest?" Eddie wasn't sure about the prospect of wandering forever as a ghost, stuck between life and death.

Franklin spread his arms in a 'we don't seem to have a choice' gesture.

"No, I don't have much choice either," Eddie gloomily agreed.

A thoughtful moment fell between them.

"It's just come to me there might be someone in the house who maybe could help you," Jeremiah broke the silence, grabbing Eddie's immediate attention. "Not sure though."

"Who?" Eddie insisted.

"I was sneaking about the house when Albright arrived this morning," he began. "Before he saw you, I heard him having an argument with someone about what he was doing."

"Ssh," Franklin interrupted, raising his hand as if sensing something. "One of Benson's henchmen is coming." Now Jeremiah picked up on it too.

"We'd best be off, or they might lock you up seeing us with you." In a second both spirits vanished.

Seconds later another figure materialised near Eddie, the same rough looking spirit who'd arrived to herd him the last time he'd been at the cottage.

"I hope you're not thinking of leaving us," the spectre snarled. "Mr Benson would not be pleased." In a moment, he too dissolved into the air.

Eddie hadn't thought of being so stupid as to try and leave the grounds by simply walking out with spectral eyes spying to locate him virtually all the time. The times he was able to communicate with Franklin and Jeremiah were precious. And no doubt they only appeared when they could detect the brief moments when he wasn't under surveillance.

He made his way back to the house, bolstered by Jeremiah's words of hope that someone at the property might be able to help him escape. But who? Just as the boy was coming to the reveal, one of Benson's parasites came. How could he discover the person or spirit there who could help? Perhaps it was one of Albright's people in the control centre. Eddie had the feeling they were human.

Only the spirit Betty had shown any sign of friendship, but she had been disappeared it seemed. By the time he reached the house, the spark of hope had flickered out.

Back in his room, he paced up and down, still wrestling with the puzzle. If he randomly approached someone who he thought might be an ally and it turned out to be wrong, in the few hours left to him, total confinement in a room would leave no opportunity to find a way before his brain was removed.

Eddie was pulled from his desperate thoughts by a knock on the door. Roberts stood there when he opened it.

"You're late for lunch," he announced," but I can bring a light refreshment to your room if you so wish."

The butler's formal tone grated. There was Eddie trying to think his way out of execution and his mind becoming enslaved, while this robotic sounding idiot harped on about meals. Holding back the insults he felt like throwing at him he closed the door.

THAT evening Eddie yearned for Jeremiah to make an appearance, hoping the boy would explain who in the house might be an ally in helping him flee. But as time passed, the spirit never came.

He laid back on the bed. The stress made him feel weary, though sleep was not going to provide a refuge tonight. Time was too short to be wasted on rest. He had to come up with something, or at least try, even if it failed.

Eddie glanced at his wristwatch. It was nearly eleven o'clock. He sat up on the bed, deciding a walk outside in the night air might refresh his mind. As he stood up, there was a knock on the door.

Surely it couldn't be the butler again calling about something ridiculous. No that was unlikely as Eddie now knew the domestic servants would be shut down for the night. Nor was it likely to be Jeremiah, who didn't need an invite to enter the room, appearing whenever he pleased.

Eddie crossed to the door and cautiously opened it. Edith stood there.

"Can I come in?" she whispered, as if anxious not to be overheard. Eddie glowered at her. This was the woman who was guilty of helping her husband to monstrously enslave people for their own selfish motives.

"What do you want?" he growled, ready to shut the door in her face.

"I want to apologise to you," she replied, her haughty, dominant manner stripped away.

"You what?" Eddie stared in disbelief, then narrowed his eyes, suspicious he was being duped as a naive fool. He began to close the door.

"No," Edith insisted, pressing her hand on it. "I know you don't trust me and I can't blame you. But I must talk to you. I don't have much time." Her eyes gleamed pleadingly. It weakened Eddie's resolve.

"Alright," he relented. "Come in for a minute, but I don't want to spend any longer with you." He widened the door gap to let her in.

"Close it quickly," she urged. "I don't want them to hear anything on the second floor." Eddie was mystified by her request, but obeyed.

"What do you want to apologise for?" he asked tersely, still suspicious of some deception buried in the so called contrition.

Edith frowned, lowering her gaze as if struggling to confess guilt of a crime.

"I want to apologise for all the misery I've caused you," she looked up, wide eyes pleading forgiveness. "And for all the dreadful things I've done to others."

Eddie stood totally confused. Her emotion seemed genuine, and it clashed with his belief that she was a hard hearted woman with no feeling for the distress she caused to anyone else.

"I don't want to see you killed and your brain removed," Edith continued her outpouring, seeming genuine in the sentiment. But Eddie remained suspicious. She'd fed him lies and half truths before.

"You've murdered people with your husband for the sake of your grisly experiments and creating slave labour." Eddie's frustration erupted at being held prisoner for them to slaughter him. He fought hard to contain his fury. "And now you come here all sorrowful for what you've done. Why in God's name should I believe you?"

"Let me at least explain to you how I was drawn into all this wickedness," Edith begged.

Eddie wasn't sure there would be any good reason to exonerate the woman for what she'd done, but felt prepared to listen to a pathetic excuse, no doubt. After that he'd boot her out. He indicated the chair at the writing desk, while he sat on the bed.

"I think you know I met my husband at the hospital where we worked," she began. "I was there to improve computer IT so that surgeons could delve more deeply into areas of the brain." Her eyes grew distant for a moment as the memory of the time came back to her.

"We worked closely, and over time Dr Albright invited me here, on a strictly confidential agreement, to view the collection of brains that his surgeon ancestors had preserved for future research when technology had improved.

Eddie listened with interest, but had heard nothing so far that released her from any guilt.

"I was absolutely fascinated that minds that had lived so many years before were just waiting to be tapped into. To hear how they had lived in their own time." Edith's face brightened as the excitement she'd felt at the prospect came back to her.

"We began working secretly together over a number of years, combining our skills here, and eventually we had our first success, reviving not only the brain, but assembling a person with the attributes of what we call ghosts, rather than an actual human." Edith paused, thinking about the thrill of the moment. "That was Mulch, our head gardener."

Then, as if struck suddenly with a heavy blow, her head dropped and she remained gazing at the floor for a few moments.

Eddie wondered if she had finished the story of boasting about her achievements with her husband. She had still shown no sign of repentance. He began to rise from the bed to usher her out. Next second Edith looked up, fixing him with an intense stare. Eddie thought the woman was about to spring at him, until he realised her eyes were reflecting intense turmoil in her mind.

"We went on to revive other people through their brains, and I saw it as an incredible step forward for the world," Edith continued. "If someone had perished in an accident before their time, as long as the brain was intact, we could bring them back into the world. Of course, they couldn't live exactly the same as a human, but much of their life would be restored, retaining thoughts and emotions much as in life." The inspiring prospect cheered her again, before the next thought arrived.

"But," she directed a troubled gaze at Eddie, "my husband did not want to reveal the achievement to the world. He began to talk about the possibility of hiring out the ones we'd restored to work for wealthy people. That it could net us a fortune. It seemed using them as servants here was not enough for him. Then he wanted to increase the workforce." She shook her head. "And for that it would mean taking lives over time of innocents like yourself."

Eddie, who had first thought that she'd come to try and persuade him that becoming part of the couple's unholy entourage would not be as bad as he thought, now began to see that Edith was genuinely growing upset.

"I was entranced by the man," she continued. "God, I was actually persuaded to go along with his plan, overcome by his amazing skill as a brain surgeon, and trapped by my own vanity of what I had helped him achieve." Edith clasped her brow as if searing pain had struck.

"I actually helped him in his murderous activity of luring people like you, who've fallen on hard times and are friendless, so they wouldn't be easily traceable." She looked at Eddie earnestly. "But now I've had enough! I cannot carry on helping him to kill innocents."

Edith's catharsis was palpable. If this was an act, thought Eddie, she would certainly win awards as a brilliant actor.

"What time is it?" Edith suddenly asked. Eddie glanced at his watch.

"Eleven twenty."

"I must get back."

"Get back?" Eddie sounded puzzled.

"Back to what we call our control centre. The monitors are constantly covered to make sure there are no problems."

Eddie recalled the young man and woman at the screens when Albright had given him the ghoulish tour.

"Who are those two young people I saw in that room when your husband showed me round?" he asked.

"Medical students," Edith replied as she rose from the chair to leave. "Them and two others come to stay here, rotating with another four students every couple of weeks. They're part of my husband's team at the hospital, and when not on monitoring duty they can continue to study and take recreation."

Eddie remembered the night when he heard two men talking in the room on the second floor during his search of the house.

"They are all sworn to secrecy about the activities here," explained Edith. "My husband has promised them he will use his influence to make sure they get top hospital jobs when they qualify." She paused, looking grim. "But I fear they will end up being murdered and becoming spirit servants. Then he can be sure they never let slip of what's going on."

Edith crossed quickly to the door.

"You look worried. In a bit of a hurry," observed Eddie.

"I told the students monitoring the control room that I'd take over from them for half-an-hour, while they had a short break. If I'm not there when they come back, it'll be logged in an official register. I'm watched just as closely as everyone else here." She was about to open the door, but stopped turning back to Eddie.

"And since I had a raging argument with my husband this morning, telling him I wanted no part in killing you or anyone else in future, any indication now that I might be doing something suspicious could lead to a lot of problems for me."

"Could you help me to escape?" Eddie asked, latching on to her desire not to kill him.

"Shh," she put her finger to her lips, in case prying ears were nearby on the landing.

"I don't know," she whispered.

"Then could you arrange for me to have a favourite meal as a sort of last dinner," he pleaded.

"I could," Edith looked puzzled by the request, then realised he was expecting it to be his last good meal before her husband arrived to perform the operation.

The surgeon had said he'd be returning in a day or so, and that meant the chance of sampling a favourite meal could be gone at any time. But behind that motive, a plan was at last hatching in Eddie's mind that might prevent his execution.

"Will your husband be coming back tomorrow?" he continued to question.

"Look, I must get back," Edith was becoming agitated. "No, he'll be at the hospital all day," she said. "He'll be back the day after." The news came as short term relief for Eddie.

"Then would you arrange for me to have steak and chips, with peas, tomatoes and mushrooms, for my last dinner tomorrow night?" he asked, giving his order.

"Of course," Edith agreed.

"And could I speak to you privately sometime tomorrow?" he pleaded.

"I'll be calling round at the garage at ten thirty, to ask our chauffeur to take a package to the local post office. If you go for a stroll in that direction, we can meet as if by chance." Edith wanted to ask why he wanted the meet, but she needed urgently to return to the control centre.

It had occurred to Eddie that she must be the possible ally in the house Jeremiah had referred to, but hadn't time to reveal. The one arguing with Albright about what he was doing. No-one else came to mind, though he could never have guessed in a million years that Edith might be his saviour.

CHAPTER 12

THE following morning Eddie left for the garage, situated at the end of the hedge lined road behind the property. Approaching the brown brick building, he saw Edith handing a parcel to the chauffeur by the open garage door. The man got into the limousine and drove off, passing close by Eddie.

"We can't be long," Edith insisted as he reached her. "What do you want?"

"Can you be in your control centre when I'm being taken to the operating theatre tomorrow?" he asked.

"I'm usually there helping with a couple of students doubling as nursing staff," she replied.

"If I do something to disrupt the proceedings, could you take control of the system," Eddie probed. It would be now or never in finding out if Edith could be depended on as an ally. That is, if she really wanted to stop helping her husband kill people. If he could trust her.

"What are you planning?" her eyes narrowed with intrigue.

"I'd rather not say just yet," he replied, "I'm still working on it." Eddie had a good idea of what he had in mind, but was reluctant to fully outline it at this moment because he felt Edith would turn him down outright.

She wondered if she should just walk away. Eddie was asking her to take part in a conspiracy that he seemed reluctant to disclose. But it must obviously be a plan that would require her to betray her husband. Eddie could read her doubts from the agitated expression.

"I thought you were sick of the killing," he snarled.

"I am," Edith snapped back, her face reddening with anger

"Then if you help me we could end it," Eddie pleaded.

"What do you have in mind for me?" Edith asked, calming a little.

"If there's a distraction for a moment, could you start to close down the system, do something to destroy the brains so they couldn't be revived?"

Edith gazed at him in astonishment. What she and her husband had achieved was a masterpiece of genius. The thought of destroying it had never occurred to her.

"Not only are you asking me to do away with all the achievements me and my husband have strived so hard on for years, but also the second lease of life the system can give people if used properly." She shook her head at the prospect of doing such a thing.

"What, robbing people who lived many years ago of their right to rest in eternal peace, only to live again as slaves. And now killing people so your husband can hire them out as servants for money. How do you intend to stop him doing that?" Now Eddie's face reddened in anger.

Edith fell silent, knowing she couldn't justifiably argue against his tirade. And, of course, she didn't want to go ahead with killing the man who stood before her, or anyone else again. Her mind stood on a tipping point.

"There is something I can do to shut down the system, but it would require any distraction to go on for at least ten minutes," she replied quietly, knowing for all her hard work and endeavours, she and her husband had created a process that in the right hands could benefit people, but in the wrong hands could be abused without limit. In her eagerness to achieve, and love for her husband, she had blinded herself to the corrupt possibilities.

"I think ten minutes should be okay," said Eddie.

"Well it's never been done before, obviously, so I can't be absolutely precise," Edith warned. Given that Eddie had no other plan in mind, he'd have to hope he could cause a distraction for that long.

"I must get back now," Edith began to walk away.

"One other thing," Eddie called. She turned.

"Could you distract Benson and his heavies from looking out for me today?" he pleaded. She frowned.

"I couldn't do that. I may be the person to run this place in my husband's absence, but Benson is highly trusted by my husband. And after my argument with him about not wanting to go on with killing, any request that might interfere with Benson's guard duties would raise suspicion," she explained.

Her reply was a disappointment. Another crucial part of his plan also depended on distracting Benson's watchers away from him for a while too.

"It's just that I was hoping to talk to Franklin and Jeremiah," he revealed. "They might be able to help," he told her.

"Ah, those two," Edith threw back her head. "They're like a couple of outlaws. We thought we'd rid ourselves of them by destroying their brains, but it didn't work. I think it's because we ripped out their electrical connections instead of introducing toxins and cutting the power more slowly. Instead we created two real ghosts," she laughed ironically, and walked off.

Eddie watched as she disappeared round the bend in the road, and wondered if she might have second thoughts about helping him. He was asking a great deal from her.

EDDIE wanted Benson and his lackeys to be elsewhere for a while so he could fit the final piece of the jigsaw into his plan. It was a plan where so many of the pieces could go missing.

It would have been better if Edith could have called off his watchers, but now as he made his way to the derelict cottage, he could only pray for a brief moment of being un-observed, and the friendly spirits hopefully appearing.

Sitting on an intact section of garden wall, he waited patiently. Twenty minutes passed, and still there was no sign of them.

He stood up and began pacing up and down on the grass. He repeated the sitting and pacing procedure several times, but still the spirits made no appearance. He began to doubt they'd arrive. They usually detected him here, but there was no guarantee.

Eddie decided to change tactic and try his luck by going to the cremation building where he knew they sometimes appeared.

It took him quarter-of-an-hour at a fast walking pace to arrive, and when he saw the square structure with its pro-truding chimney tube, terror tore through him at the thought his own body minus brain, might soon be consumed in the furnace flames if his escape plan didn't work.

He waited for an hour, pacing the setting and occasionally calling their names. Eventually in growing despair he decided the spirits were not going to show up, so he took the decision to leave.

Gloom clouded his thoughts as he returned to the house, he was determined to go ahead with his plan, but it was less likely to succeed without some further help from Franklin and Jeremiah.

Eddie was about to enter the front door, when he heard a voice from behind.

"I don't know what you're up to," Benson called from the bottom of the entrance steps, "but don't think I'm not watching." The snarling threat matched his vicious, narrowed eyes as Eddie turned to face him. His thoughts of being able to escape began to fade further.

TRUE to her word, Edith had given the order to provide Eddie with his requested last steak dinner that evening.

As he sat in the loneliness of the large dining room, which would have been filled with much feasting and laughter once upon a time, his appetite was not in the mood for consuming a meal that in the past he'd have relished. He hoped it wouldn't be his last meal as a human being, but it might.

Edith had also provided vintage wine, and the desire to get drunk to ease the tension he was suffering became tempting, but he declined to touch a drop. He wanted to keep his mind fresh for tomorrow. From the meal, there was only one consolation he'd derived, causing him to raise a brief smile as he mounted the stairs to his room.

Settling on the bed, he began reading his book for a while. After half-an-hour, and his mind hardly taking in the storyline, he decided to undress and get into bed. Reaching across he turned out the bedside light.

After maybe ten or twenty minutes of resting in the darkness, and unable to get some sleep, he heard the chair scrape at the writing table.

"Is that you Jeremiah?" he called. Suddenly the boy's figure glowed his presence at the end of the bed. Eddie reached out and switched on the bedside light.

"Just for old times sake," the lad grinned.

"For God's sake can you ever stop behaving stupidly!" Eddie cried angrily, sitting up.

"Sorry," the boy's smile dropped into a guilty frown.

Then Eddie felt guilty too. He was fond of Jeremiah, but his childish ways could be extremely annoying.

"Okay." Eddie softened his tone. "You just startled me."

The spirit youngster's smile returned, relieved at being forgiven.

"Can't stay long," he said. "I only just managed to slip past Benson's watchers. They're keeping a very close guard on the place, just in case you try to escape."

"I went to the cottage hoping to see you and your dad," Eddie explained, "and then to that dreadful cremation place."

"Me and dad know," answered the boy. "We was there hiding. But Benson had a couple of his heavies keeping an eye on you, so we couldn't talk."

"I think Edith might help me to escape," Eddie announced.

"That's who I heard arguing with Albright about not wanting to help him kill people anymore. But we had to scarper the last time we met, just before I could tell you her name. Remember?" reminded Jeremiah. "So you found out she might help?"

"She came to me to confess she no longer wanted to do it," explained Eddie, "and said she was sorry for what was happening to me."

"Edith doesn't really run the place, Benson is Albright's man, trusts him more than his wife." Jeremiah knew the workings of the house well.

"Anyway, I've got to go soon before they find me here," the boy changed tack. "What did you want to see us for?"

"Could you and your father remain as near as possible to the house tomorrow?" asked Eddie.

"Well I can slip past Benson's watchdogs unseen now and again, but me and dad would be seen straight away if we got near the place. There's a lot of guards around it. Invisible spirits can see other invisible spirits, and stop them as if they were solid like humans if they catch them," Jeremiah explained.

Eddie frowned. The youngster could see he was troubled.

"What have you got in mind?"

"Albright is going to operate on me tomorrow," he said, "or should I say murder me."

"Bastard," the boy swore in disgust. Another time Eddie would have told the lad not to use that language, but couldn't fault the sentiment right now.

"I have a plan to cause a distraction tomorrow, which might draw Benson's watchers outside to rush into the house," Eddie described part of his plan. "If you and your father can keep a reasonable distance from the property without being seen, you might have a chance to come inside and help. I need to keep as much distraction going on as possible for about ten minutes or more in their control room."

"Well dad said we'd help you get away from this hell hole if we could," the boy replied, "and if you give us a chance to get in there tomorrow, we will. I can probably sneak a bit nearer to the place than dad, and keep an eye out. Then call I'll him if we can get in." He paused for a moment.

"How are you going to cause this distraction? the spirit asked.

"I've got an action in mind, and Edith has said she'll help me end the horror of the house by closing down the system," Eddie explained.

Jeremiah stared in amazement.

"Are you sure she said that?" the spirit demanded confirmation.

"Yes," Eddie replied, looking puzzled by the question. "Why do you ask?"

"She's a spirit too," announced the boy. "To prove her idea that you could create spirits using the brains of dead people by her system, she volunteered to have her brain removed by Albright for the first experiment and have it connected up."

Eddie's eyes widened as the information sank in.

"When they were happy it all worked okay, Mulch was the first one after her to be revived from the older brains in the collection," continued Jeremiah. "It was him who told us about it."

Now doubt surfaced in Eddie's mind. Would Edith really finish herself off by closing down the system, or would she choose self-preservation at the last minute? Would she prefer to continue existing as a spirit, or plunge herself into oblivion?

CHAPTER 13

EDDIE hardly slept that night. He tried to think of happier times in attempts to keep his nerves under control, but it was hard not to be drawn back again to thoughts of tomorrow. Would his plan work?

Memories of being together with his former partner, Steph, who'd left him because of his reckless gambling, filled much of his mind. If only he hadn't been so stupid, they'd still be together, and he'd never have encountered Albright.

Now he realised even more how much he loved and needed her, missed her. If he could have another chance. That small word 'if'. How big it is in reality, he considered.

A light sleep did eventually take him, only soon to be interrupted by a knock on the door. He reached for his watch on the bedside table. Seven o'clock.

"Who is it?" he called.

"The lady Edith wants to know what you desire for breakfast?" Roberts called.

"Nothing. Just coffee in my room."

"Very well."

Eddie dressed, then soon came another knock at the door. Roberts entered and placed the drink on the writing desk.

"Mr Benson wishes you to meet him in the hall in half-an-hour," the butler announced in his usual monotone, and left the room.

As Eddie sipped his coffee, he had to take extra care not to spill it, his hands beginning to tremble in fear of his impending fate. There was nothing certain about how events would unfold.

BENSON seemed to be attempting to raise an unaccustomed smile as they met in the hall. Eddie felt it was more likely to be a smirk of satisfaction, with the spirit looking forward to his forthcoming fate.

"Follow me," Benson ordered.

They entered the hall door under the staircase, and made their way along the passageway down into the control centre. Now Eddie's nerves soared to a new pitch of terror, with the thought of being executed growing closer if his plan didn't work.

Inside the centre, two of Albright's medical students sat monitoring activity on the screens. Benson led him into an adjoining room with a table and chair to one side, and a tall cabinet on the other. Benson opened the cabinet and took out a hospital gown.

"Undress and put this on," he commanded.

Eddie began to panic. He'd hoped Edith would have been at one of the monitors in the control centre, ready to shut down the system once he'd caused a distraction. It seemed she had changed her mind. Hope for him was slipping away.

"No, I won't put the gown on!" Eddie shouted. "No, no, no, you're all bloody murderers," he continued to shout at the top of his voice.

Benson was about to restrain him and strip his clothes off, when Albright and Edith, dressed in medical gowns, rushed in through a connecting door from the operating theatre. They were followed by a student.

"What's all this?" Albright demanded.

"I'm not going to let you kill me and make me your servant," Eddie blasted.

"Alright, calm down," the surgeon's tone softened. He approached Eddie, raising a friendly smile. "If you don't want to go ahead with the procedure, we'll cancel it," he said.

Eddie was confused. Surely the surgeon wanted to extract his brain, it was the whole point of him being lured to the house? He deeply wanted to believe this reprieve from execution, and began to relax a little.

"Grab him Benson, so we can get the tranquilliser in!" Albright's face swiftly narrowed into an evil snarl, as Benson reached to grab his victim.

But Eddie acted swiftly too. In seconds he reached into the waist band of his trousers and drew out a steak knife, the one he'd successfully sneaked out unnoticed from his meal last night.

Before Benson could grasp him, Eddie plunged the blade with all his might into Albright's heart. Blood rapidly seeped into his medical gown forming a large red patch on his chest. The surgeon staggered back, the weapon protruding from him. He stared in shocked amazement at the knife, then Eddie, before toppling stone dead on to his back.

Eddie didn't know what retribution now lay in store for him, but the triumph of seeing the vile medic destroyed, filled him with overwhelming joy.

Edith stared at her lifeless husband, but was not moved to kneel by his side in bitter sorrow and tears, or even try to see if she could save him. It was as if heavy chains shackling her soul had been unlocked, that there was a path to redemption.

Benson knelt to check his master's body, completely stunned by the incident, blaming himself for not making sure Eddie wasn't carrying a weapon. His anger was set to explode, and take vengeance for the killing. But events were beginning to unfold elsewhere.

Edith evaporated from the room to re-appear in the control centre and shoved a student at one of the screens off his chair. She began frantically tapping on the touchpad, causing sirens to start blasting.

The spirit guards monitoring the house outside immediately materialised in the room, looking for instructions to deal with the emergency summons.

The student who'd been pushed away tried to regain control of his screen, but now Eddie had rushed into the room and began grappling with him, throwing him on the floor. The young woman student at the monitor beside Edith desperately tried to override further commands she could see her inputting, but Edith's superior programming skills were way beyond the student's ability to counter them.

Benson materialised in the room, and attempted to stop Edith. Eddie grabbed the spirit now in its solid form. He knew it would be fruitless to try and overcome such a powerful enemy, but hoped it would cause a temporary obstruction.

The half dozen ghost guards looked at each other in confusion, not sure who they should be tackling and waiting for an instruction. Benson had easily pushed Eddie aside, but Edith, with spirit power that equalled his own, was proving more difficult to remove. He turned to command the guards to remove her from her seat while he took stock of the situation.

Franklin and Jeremiah suddenly appeared among the commotion, now that the outside was no longer under guard. Benson immediately issued an order for his team to leave Edith and tackle them instead. The chaos was causing him confusion, not sure what event should be taking priority to focus on. The guards were also thrown into confusion as Franklin and his son dodged around the room running up the walls and across the ceiling, avoiding their opponents.

The young man who Edith had unseated made another attempt to remove her, but this time she dissolved, continuing to operate as a phantom, leaving her human attacker unable to grasp her or get access to the touchpad. Then materialising again, she swiftly dealt him a hard elbow blow in the stomach, sending him staggering back.

A few seconds later she voluntarily vacated the seat, turning to survey the total disarray. It gave her delight to see the control freak Benson completely at a loss on how to deal with the chaos. She'd never liked him, but had needed to put on an act to fit the formality her husband demanded.

Eddie watched too, grateful his spirit friends had been true to their word and come to his aid when the guards had been summoned to the centre.

Benson noticed that Edith was no longer at the monitor.

"Stop!" he ordered his men, bringing the chase for Franklin and Jeremiah to a halt. He stared across the room at Edith.

"What have you done?" he demanded.

She made no reply and just smiled, glancing across at the brains suspended in the tanks, which were now filling with a dark yellow fluid.

Benson followed the line of her sight, turning to see the liquid in the tanks behind becoming discoloured.

"What have you done?" His repeated demand now had the cry of panic. Still Edith made no reply, continuing to smile.

He vanished to instantly reappear at the terminal where she'd been working. He saw a graph line that should have remained below the safe level marker. It was now in the red critical zone. An alarm should have sounded to signal for rapid remedial action, but Edith had disarmed it.

The young woman beside the terminal Edith had used was frantically trying to reverse the process without success.

"Stop this happening!" Benson shrieked at Edith. "Have you lost you're mind?"

She laughed, gazing at the tank which contained her brain and now disappearing from view in the growing murky solution.

"No, I think I've found it," she replied.

Getting nowhere with her, Benson turned his fury towards Eddie, the only other human in the room beside the students. He'd been so keen to bring him under his total control as a spirit.

Eddie gauged the hatred in his eyes as the spirit began to approach, and was terrified he might be torn to bits in a frenzied attack. He backed towards the door instinctively to escape. Jeremiah saw the peril and moved in to help as Benson grabbed Eddie by his shirt collar, releasing a hand briefly to whack the boy away with a swipe.

Now Benson gripped Eddie's throat. If he wasn't going to be killed one way by Albright, then he would by another. Eddie began to shudder as massive pressure closed his windpipe. Franklin moved in to save him. But the grip began to ease before rescue was necessary.

Benson released him and started to step back, a confused look on his face. He turned to see Edith still standing beside the monitor, her smile becoming broader.

With the oxygen supply restored to Eddie, he now watched as his tormentor seemed to start fading, gradually becoming translucent, decreasing into a wispy form and then completely evaporating.

The guards, who were none the wiser in the confusion, still wondered precisely what actions they should be taking. Staring in awe, they witnessed their leader fade away.

As they gazed, the same fate began affecting them. For a few seconds they looked at each other with puzzled expressions, as if trying to understand something happening to them. Then they dissolved into nothing.

Edith remained intact. Eddie wondered if she'd engineered it so she would be the sole survivor. He took in the beauty of her chestnut brown eyes and honey coloured hair touching her shoulders. The white short sleeved blouse, with the purple heart choker, and wine red skirt outfit she'd worn when he first arrived.

"I did love my husband, and that memory remains," she told him. "We were a brilliant team, and what we did could have re-united loved one's from beyond the veil of death." She paused. "But I blindly allowed myself to be drawn into the evil purposes he'd intended."

Edith glanced around, reminiscing on the couple's unique endeavours, and the brain tanks now completely yellowed by the destructive fluid she'd introduced. Then she looked again at Eddie.

"I forgive you for killing my husband, and I understand you had no alternative." She evaporated into a mist and was gone.

Now only Eddie, Franklin and Jeremiah remained in the centre, with the two medical students who'd been at the monitor controls, and the female student who was going to assist with the operation.

Looks of panic and confusion crossed between them, totally confounded by what had happened and fearing they might come under attack from the trio now staring hard at them. They seemed to make an unspoken decision about their options and speedily fled from the room.

"Seems like we're the only spirits left to reside in this place now," said Jeremiah. "The rest of Albright's creations are probably in another place somewhere."

"Well, wherever they are now, some of them should be down there," Eddie pointed at the floor. "Be happy we've got rid of a bloody evil regime."

"Yeah, good riddance to it," Franklin backed the sentiment.

"Me and dad are really glad you didn't become another of Albright's slaves," said Jeremiah. "But we will miss you being here."

Eddie was finding it hard to take on board that he was actually being told he would be missed by ghosts. Harcourt Grange would remain as the most surreal experience of his life.

"It's been a pleasure to have helped you," Franklin held out his hand to shake Eddie's. "We'll probably be staying in this part of the world, so come and visit us sometime. We'll keep an eye out at the derelict cottage."

Eddie wasn't sure he'd ever want to revisit the place. One visit was enough.

Both spirits smiled at him, then dissolved.

A wave of loneliness struck him when they'd gone. He stood alone in that dreaded room, and the reality of normal life came flooding in. He was still homeless, had no job and no immediate prospects. But mostly, there remained the rift with his ex-partner Steph, and his love for her undiminished.

As he exited the control centre to leave the property, an overwhelming sensation of emptiness now replaced the feeling of unseen spirits and foreboding that had perpetually gripped him during his confinement.

Stepping outside the building, he looked across at the ornamental garden, now devoid of gardeners busily working at flower beds and trimming hedges. Edith had terminated the whole show, including herself.

He wondered if all of them would become ghosts like Franklin and Eddie, forever haunting the place.

Then he remembered Edith telling him it had happened because she'd terminated their brains too quickly, leading to that result. She'd enacted a slower process of wholesale termination just now, presumably for all the generated spirits not to end up as rootless spirits.

But what did Eddie know about those things? As long as he didn't have to stay there to find out, he was happy. His only hope was that the Albright and Benson had gone to hell. At least Edith had repented.

Now the prospect for his own future came to the fore again. He still had enough left from the money the surgeon had given him to travel to his home by train. He remembered the limousine was kept at the property's garage, and made his way there. But it was missing. If the chauffeur was also a spirit, he may have dissolved out on a job somewhere.

Eddie needed a cab to take him to the station, since he had no idea where it was or how far. The local village inn, The Royal Oak, came to mind, where Benson had violently hauled him out when Eddie had first attempted to escape.

Benson, he recalled, had told customers he was retrieving an escaped psychiatric patient. Would the barman, whose phone Eddie had been about to use for calling a cab, remember him and call the police? He'd have to chance it.

Hope to find a different barman serving whose phone he could try and borrow.

Trekking the route he'd previously taken across the fields to the village, Eddie couldn't help feeling the sensation that Benson or his henchmen were following him, ready to appear any second and force him back. It took a while for the feeling to start fading. After all, he reasoned, he'd seen their brains being destroyed and them disappearing.

He thought about Edith. For all her bad ways, he'd felt attracted to her as a woman, and admired her brilliance. If only the achievements could have been put to good use, though he wasn't sure how many people would want to exist as half ghosts.

Reaching the village he began walking towards the high street to reach the inn. Coming towards him on the pavement an elderly man carrying a shopping bag stopped to chat with him.

"Enjoying a walk?" he began.

"Yes," Eddie quickly replied, ready to continue his journey.

"Where you off to?" the man continued.

"The inn to call a cab. I need to get to the station."

"Oh you don't need to call a cab. Fit looking chap like you could get there walking. Save money. It's only a mile away. Otherwise there's a bus in an hour."

Eddie brightened at the news. He wouldn't have to risk running the gauntlet at the inn.

"If you walk," said the man, pointing along the pavement, "a little way down there, then turn left on to the footpath, it goes straight to the station. Short cut you see." He was about to continue the conversation, but getting out of the area was Eddie's prime objective.

"Thank you," he replied, and made his way. The old man's eyes followed him for a moment, then he walked on.

The footpath led through a wood. Once again the feeling of being followed came on him. Was the old man some spirit ruse from the house, sent to direct him along here, so that Benson could grab him without prying eyes and excuses for apprehending him. Dismissing the thought, Eddie feared the paranoia of Harcourt Grange would trouble him on and off for some time.

CHAPTER 14

THE feeling of immense triumph filled Eddie's soul, enjoying his freedom and seeing trees, pastures and villages flash past on the train taking him back to his home town.

Then gradually the consequences of what he'd done began to cloud his mind. Sooner or later Albright's body would be discovered.

The police would run DNA tests to seek clues. Eddie's genetic markers would be all over the place, including the possessions he'd left behind in order to leave the horror as soon as possible.

Eddie had no criminal record so DNA links would be unlikely, unless some relative had broken the law with his or her marker now on file. Then the police might get round to interviewing and taking a sample from him to compare with things found at Harcourt Grange.

There would probably be CCTV at the station, and the police might find him with publicity, if looking to interview him about visiting the area. But often those cameras were not active. He'd have to hope that was the case.

Then the students could be a link, if the police traced them and grilled them for information. Did they know his name, or was he just another faceless victim trapped by the surgeon?

Eddie began to break out in a cold sweat as the possibilities gripped him. A charge of murder would result in a long prison stretch, swapping one incarceration for another. Offering a defence that Albright was killing people to create spirits from their brains, would likely raise more laughs than provide justice.

As the train pulled into his home town, Eddie's former overpowering joy had gone. His next problem was finding a place to stay. The money left from what Albright had given him was nearly gone, just enough to buy budget takeaways for a couple of days.

The thought of bedding down overnight in the park where he'd met the surgeon terrified him, but since there was no chance of meeting the evil bastard there again, it was the best option. The park was the only place in the town that offered sufficient foliage to hide.

He bought a takeaway burger and chips, then made his way to the park to find a bench to eat them, but took the opposite direction on the path to find one far enough away from the Albright bench.

Approaching a seat, he suddenly dropped the takeaway bag. Staring in horror he thought he saw Albright seated there, glancing at him. Then the apparition, or imagining was gone.

"For God's sake, is this man going to haunt me forever!" Eddie loudly exclaimed, causing some nearby strollers to eye him as if he wasn't right in the head, before quickly moving on.

Eddie picked up the takeaway bag and speedily moved on too, deciding the park was no longer where he planned to spend the night.

He left and made his way to the town square, with shops and cafes bordering it on three sides, a fountain at the centre and the grand, dark brick council office building dominating the fourth.

Sitting on a bench overlooking the setting, he delved into the nearly cold takeaway and began eating. As well as all the other problems now dominating his mind, homelessness presently took the lead.

A young woman crossing the square approached the bench and sat on the far end from him. She took a phone from her bag and soon engaged in conversation.

Eddie glanced at her, taking in the woman's cropped auburn hair, snub nose on her side outline, and tie wrap red jacket over a dark blue dress.

FRANKLIN and Jeremiah appeared in the basement control centre, now left abandoned after the riotous confrontation. The tanks had become deeply discoloured, the liquid almost black. A couple of the monitor screens continued to display data in their redundant state.

Viewing the setting was not the spirits' motive for being there. Jeremiah showed his father to a side room, both gliding through the door to see a desk and a shelf above containing books. A wood block strip on the wall held several keys on hooks.

Jeremiah selected one with a longer length than the others, which he'd seen used in a particular setting during one of his spying sessions.

At the rear of the property a large stack of petrol cans were kept in a storeroom to maintain generator back-up in power cuts. The spirits had learned it was a highly volatile liquid. Unlocking the secure metal door, father and son invisibly glided back and forth carrying them into the house.

The property was largely a wooden structure, and the spirits painstakingly spread the contents in the rooms, down the stairways, and throughout the control centre. After dousing the kitchen with the accelerant, Jeremiah turned on the gas rings and let the fumes fill the room before igniting it.

The combination of petrol vapour and gas combined to create a ferocious explosion, blasting the kitchen into oblivion, and violently bursting through the doors, walls and ceiling. Instantly the flames raged upwards through the house, while following a vapour trail down into the basement. The genius technology Albright and his wife had soured into evil, was consigned to the hell fire it justly deserved.

Both spirits wandered through the conflagration impervious to the flames, and relished with great satisfaction the wholesale destruction being wrought. Never again could the property be used for ill. In the distance, the distinct wailing of fire engine sirens could be heard approaching.

EDDIE finished his takeaway as the woman sitting on the park bench nearby continued her chat on the phone. A few minutes later the conversation ended. She replaced the phone in her handbag and stood up to leave.

The thought that had been surfacing in Eddie's mind, but which he'd been reluctant to put into action, became more pressing as the woman was about to walk away.

"Excuse me," he called to her. She turned staring at him quizzically in his creased clothes and trainers, which were covered in dried mud from when he'd traipsed across the fields to the village.

She was wary of his general unkempt appearance, though felt fairly secure with many people criss-crossing the square.

"It's okay," said Eddie, noting her caution. "I'm not some weirdo. It's just I've run into some difficulties and lost my phone. I need to contact my friend and ask them to collect me," he paused, eyeing her pleadingly. "Could I use your phone to call them?"

The woman looked at him suspiciously, fearing if she gave him her phone, he'd run off with it.

"Look I'll give you my wrist watch to hold," Eddie began unstrapping it. "It's probably more valuable than the phone, a Rolex." Steph had bought the watch for him as a birthday present, and he'd not risk being parted from it unless he was desperate.

The woman remained reluctant, but took the offering and examined it. Satisfied, she popped it into her handbag, and handed her phone to Eddie.

He dithered for a moment, trying to remember Steph's number, relying normally on autodial stored on his own phone. Remembering, he called her. Several ring tones gave way to messaging. Should he leave a message or not? No, it would be better for her to hear him directly. A disembodied voice mail wouldn't express what he wanted to say in the same way.

"Thanks," he handed back the phone, as the woman returned his watch and left.

Since another night of sleeping in the park was out of the question, Eddie decided to opt for a derelict factory building in the town, where the homeless bedded down. The realisation he'd reached such depths was hard to bear. He'd have to apply for benefit to keep body and soul together until he could find work, though looking unkempt and being homeless would not help with that, and the money Albright had given him was nearly out.

Rising from the bench, he tossed the takeaway bag into a nearby bin and began leaving the square.

"Excuse me?" a voice came from behind, "were you ringing someone called Steph?" Eddie turned to see the woman whose phone he'd borrowed. He nodded. She handed him her phone.

"Who's this?" Steph asked. Eddie didn't instantly reply. The sound of her voice lifted his mood, but he wondered if she'd hang up the moment he spoke.

"Who's this?" she repeated impatiently, sounding close to ending the call.

"It's me, Eddie." There was a silence that seemed to him to last forever. "Please don't hang up. Are you still there?" The silence continued a little longer.

"Yes," Steph replied, stiffness her tone.

"I've been through absolute hell," he said, "and I've missed you so much."

"What spent every penny gambling in another hopeless attempt to win a fortune?" she sneered.

"No I haven't, and I only did that stupid thing in an attempt to save our business," he pleaded. Another silence followed.

"What have you been doing?" she asked, her voice softening a little.

"A few cash in hand jobs at some downmarket takeaways, a bit of building site jobbing. Been sleeping rough all the time, as I don't get much money for it. Hope to get better work soon."

Eddie lied, fearing Steph would finish the call if he revealed what had really been happening, ghosts, poltergeists, brains being harnessed to resurrect people from the dead. He was silent for a moment.

"Can you help me?" he pleaded. "Just put me up for a few days, so I can wash my clothes, tidy myself up?"

Steph wavered. Her love for him remained strong, despite his stupidity with the gambling strategy, but she'd experienced her own hell when the business had ended, wrecking their plans for a successful future together. Could she stand the possibility of going through that again?

"I've managed to get a bank loan instead of moving back to my parents, and now have a flat above a vacant shop where I plan to start a new business like we had before," she explained, "only offering a wider range of food this time."

Eddie concluded that with the fresh start she was making, she'd be reluctant to let him return and possibly spoil it again.

"It's okay, I understand," he said. "I wouldn't want to mess things up for you." He'd decided to drop the hope of being put up for a few days. "Wish you well with it though."

"Wait," Steph called, gauging he was about to hang up. "You can stay with me for a few days, after that decisions will have to be taken."

Was that opening a chance at redemption? Eddie's heart began pounding at the opportunity of being re-united with her, even if it turned out only briefly.

"I'm moved to Bosworth now," Steph told him. "Can you get here?"

"Not really," Eddie replied. "I'm back in Tollbridge, right now in the town square, and I don't have the train fare to travel. I could try hitch hiking though."

"Stay there. You're about 20 miles away from me, I'll come and collect you in the car," Steph announced.

Eddie handed back the phone he'd been lent. The woman gave a wry smile, making it obvious she'd got the gist of the conversation. Perhaps for the first time in his relationship with Steph, he now realised just how lucky he was to have met her.

CHAPTER 15

THE apartment above the shop in Bosworth was comfortable enough, with a kitchen dining area, living room and decent sized bedroom. Steph had ideas for more furnishings and decoration in the flat, but first she'd ordered fittings for the shop below, which presently lay bare after the previous sandwich bar owner had cleared the premises. Quickly setting up the business was key to her plans.

"Thank you," said Eddie, coming into the kitchen from the bedroom after showering and putting on a clean shirt and trousers, which Steph had stopped to buy for him on the way back. She was finishing frying omelettes and serving them on to plates, shortly joining Eddie at the dining table.

Afterwards Steph opened a bottle of wine, and they sat together on the living room sofa chatting. Eddie felt guilty embroidering lies of his recent odd jobbing experiences and being homeless during their separation. But how could he believably tell her about the events at Harcourt Grange? She'd think him insane.

A spell of thoughtful silence fell between them as they sipped their wine.

"I've been considering whether to give you another chance," Steph broke the stillness. "Perhaps a probation period," she took another sip. "That's if you're interested."

"I was very stupid, but I honestly believed at the time that I could use gambling to claw our way out of debt," Eddie didn't directly answer her question, feeling the confession served as a way of healing the rift between them, so they could be together again.

"If only you'd told me earlier, I would have injected some money left to me by a wealthy aunt," she replied. "It was a big sum and earning good interest. There for a rainy day," Steph shook her head.

"Instead I had to use a large part of it to get us out of the shit and pay off the mortgage repayments debt. Then I put the shop up for sale to clear the rest of the mortgage, because staying there would only be a bad memory for me. There's an interested buyer, and it'll hopefully be sold soon."

She stared at Eddie disapprovingly. "Fortunately I had enough money left over to take a lease on this flat and the shop for a new start."

Eddie leaned forward on the sofa burying his head in shame. Steph was satisfied she'd left him in no doubt about the devastating disruption he'd caused in her life, and the fury she'd felt. Placing her hand on his shoulder, she gently raised him up.

"For some reason, God know why, I still love you though," she slipped her arm round his shoulder and pulled him close. Their lips met.

"Come on," she said as they parted, "it's time for bed."

A FULL moon illuminated the bedroom curtains casting enough silvery light for Eddie to see the room layout. He thought he'd been awoken by the scrape of a chair, and he sat up to glance across at the dressing table.

The chair stood a little way from the footwell. Had it been tucked in when they'd gone to bed? He couldn't be certain. Furniture positioning was not a priority on the couple's minds when they'd bedded down.

Over the next few days they discussed plans for the new shop, the layout and the planned increase in the food and drink offerings. They were genuinely happy to be reunited, though Steph was now taking charge of the finances.

Settling on the sofa one evening, she watched the television, while Eddie beside her scrolled through some news pages on the laptop. He was eager to find a particular item. Following a short search, he came across the story he was looking for, but was knocked back by it.

He'd been expecting to see news of the fatal stabbing of Albright at Harcourt Grange, and the grisly find of decayed brains in tanks. For days Eddie had been living in fear of the discovery, and whether the police would connect DNA sampling with him. Instead the headline took him by complete surprise.

MYSTERY INFERNO DESTROYS

MISSING SURGEON'S HOME

The article featured two side by side photos showing Harcourt Grange as it was, and the totally gutted heap of ashes it had become.

The story read:

"It was the residence of Dr Ernest Albright, a distinguished brain surgeon, and his wife Edith, a former IT consultant. Firemen searching the destroyed remains of the property have found partial remains of what appear to be human bones, although tests are yet to be conducted on them.

Dr Albright and his wife have been missing since the fire, and it is believed the bone remains may be those of the couple.

The complete destruction of the house is attributed to its mainly wooden construction, though there is a theory that an accelerant may have speeded the progress of the conflagration. At present this has not been confirmed."

Eddie stopped reading for a moment in thought. He wondered who could have started the blaze. The students? It came as great relief that the blaze had been so intense that all traces of him ever being there must have been destroyed, including evidence he stabbed Albright. They'd still find the cremation building intact. But there would be nothing there, or at the derelict cottage, to link him with the place. He continued reading:

"Melted strips of metal, believed to possibly be parts of holding tanks, have also been discovered. It is speculated that Dr Albright may have had a collection of tropical fish, but heat from the fire was so intense, any trace of what was contained in them is unlikely to have survived."

Although totally amazed at what he was reading, Eddie could not help bursting out with laughter at the line Albright may have been keeping tropical fish in the tanks.

"What are you laughing at?" asked Steph, glancing at the laptop screen. Eddie had to think fast.

"Oh, an advert popped up beside this story advertising thermal clothing. It's gone now. Thought it was a bit rich next to a story about a big fire." He could hardly tell her it was the house where he'd nearly had his brain removed, and that he'd killed the surgeon.

Steph took a glance at the article.

"Sounds a bit mysterious," she commented, and returned to watching the TV. Eddie closed the laptop and began viewing with her. A trailer came on featuring a forthcoming film about Queen Victoria.

"That reminds me," Steph began, "when I was coming in from the car with some shopping today, I saw a boy standing at the corner nearby. He was dressed in clothes that looked like he came from the Victorian era."

She paused, muting the TV for a moment as she recalled the event.

"Yes, he had a flat cap, collarless white shirt, and I think it was a brown waistcoat and black trousers," she described him.

"He smiled at me, then I put the shopping down to take out the door key. When I looked again, he was gone. Probably went round the corner on his way to a fancy dress party. There was something strange about him though. Can't think what."

Eddie smiled, looking completely composed, but inside struck by her words.

"Silly," Steph continued, "for a moment, I thought I'd seen a ghost." She laughed. "But of course, they don't really exist."

OTHER BOOKS BY THE AUTHOR

I hope you enjoyed *The Ghosts of Harcourt Grange*. If you would like to read more of my books they are listed below and available through Amazon. But first a taste of my popular novel:

DEAD SPIRITS FARM

THE PREVIOUS residents of the old farmhouse were lucky. They left just in time. The next couple to own the property were not so fortunate.

Its name, Fairview Farm, disguised a grim title that residents in the nearby village of Calbridge gave to the place. But that was one of the terrifying revelations yet to come in the unfolding story of the new owners.

Benjamin Telford, or Ben as he was known by friends and colleagues, had spent thirty years creating a successful housebuilding company. He was a hands-on man, starting as a building site labourer in his mid-twenties and eventually branching out to form his own construction business.

Now he was more office bound at High Wycombe, a busy town thirty five miles to the north west of London.

Even in his mid-fifties, Ben was still a strong, muscular man, betrayed only in age by greying hair and a furrowed brow. But his thoughts were turning towards taking an early retirement. He'd talked it over with his wife, Eleanor, on several occasions at their home situated not far from the company office.

They'd been married for twenty-five years. Ben had hired the attractive brunette with such beautifully innocent eyes shortly after he'd started his own company. Eleanor's young eyes might have looked innocent, but she was a shrewd accountant and a tempest of authority in her later role as business manager. She'd played a key role in the success of the business.

"There's an old farmhouse going cheap near a small village called Calbridge," said Ben as he sat on the sofa at home looking at properties for sale on his laptop. Eleanor sat beside him reading a book, the sound of the TV quiz show in front of them muted. She stopped reading to look across.

"It's in west Cornwall, not far from the sea," Ben continued, scrolling through the details. "Needs a bit of doing up, but I could make that my project. Might be ideal for our retirement plans."

"Wonder why it's going so cheap?" Eleanor's shrewd mind never lost its inquisitive grip, even though that young, innocent countenance had matured since with a few wrinkles. The rising tide of grey hair, however, was not to be tolerated, held back by the colouring of youthful brunette.

"Looks like someone's done work on the main farmhouse," Ben didn't appear to be taking in his wife's questioning, "but some outbuildings along the side need restoration. Might even be able to offer them as holiday lets. A bit of income." Ben had been office bound for too long. He yearned to use his practical building skills again. He turned to Eleanor.

"It's probably going cheap because of costly redevelopment work needed on the old storage outbuildings." He had been listening to his wife. "If I do it myself then the cost is a lot less."

Eleanor didn't feel entirely settled with the prospect, but it would be good if they could have an early retirement home not far from the sea in a beautiful countryside county where they'd spent holidays in the past, though this area and the village of Calbridge were unfamiliar to them. The couple decided Ben would take a few days off to visit the property and see the local estate agent.

That night Eleanor had an uneasy night's sleep. She dreamed her husband was calling for help from a doorway, his hand outstretched desperately trying to reach her, but being pulled back by some unseen force.

"What's the matter?"

She woke to see Ben sitting up beside her, wondering why she was crying out in distress.

"It's alright," she replied, rubbing her eyes, "just a bad dream."

Eleanor settled to sleep again, only to see her son, Michael, trying to comfort her in the loss of someone dear. Then her daughter Sophie joined him, dressed in sombre dark clothes, attempting to console her. Eleanor jolted waking from the dream, sitting upright on the bed. She stared into the darkness of the bedroom, the subdued glow of a street lamp shining through the curtains giving a little visibility.

"What's the matter ol' girl? What's troubling you?" For the second time Ben sat up beside her, this time placing his arm around her shoulders.

"It's okay. I'm just having some bad dreams," she rubbed her eyes again, as if that would wipe away the fear that had surfaced in her subconscious mind. "Didn't mean to disturb you."

"Probably that cheese and biscuits snack we had before going to bed," said Ben comforting her, "given you indigestion and bad dreams. Settle down my love. Everything's okay."

Her husband's warming words made Eleanor relax. She rested again, thoughts of her son Michael happily married to Australian girl, Lizzie, who he'd met when she'd come to the UK on a month long visit after graduating from university.

Michael was a whiz at accountancy, genetically inherited from his mother, and held the career qualification Lizzie planned to pursue. They clicked. He left his UK job to join her in Sydney, marrying a short time later and setting up their own business.

Eleanor missed him, but felt glad he was happy. Ben had harboured hopes that Michael would join the family business. But that's children for you he'd lamented, also glad his son was building a future.

Daughter Sophie was a single-minded woman, determined not to be drawn into distracting relationships. That is, until she met Leonard.

He was in complete contrast to the type of person everyone thought she would choose for a partner. A mild mannered man, inoffensive, non-argumentative and always happy to embrace another person's point of view. It obviously flummoxed Sophie. She had nothing to contest her fiery personality against. She fell madly in love with him, vowing always to protect him, and they'd been contentedly married for five years.

Sophie had moved from the local area too, now living a long distance away in Scotland, although not so distant as son Michael.

Eleanor drifted into sleep again, but somewhere in the back of her mind Ben's plans for the farmhouse retirement did not rest easily.

******

A COUPLE of days later Ben made the long journey to Calbridge to meet the local estate agent, Justin Turnbull. From the village he was driven to the farmhouse in the agent's car. The salesman was full of enthusiasm for the property.

"Heaps of potential," he described the place, pulling up on the farmstead's paved, red brick frontage.

Ben got out of the car and strode towards the dark oak front door. Justin caught up with him, adjusting his tie knot and smoothing his grey suit.

The original single-storey structure of the greystone farmhouse had been extended in local matching stone by the previous owner, adding first floor accommodation with a pitched slate roof.

Inside, the living room had been enlarged by demolishing the wall to an adjoining old pantry. It was a sizable area with a beamed ceiling. An inglenook fireplace added to the character of the setting.

The kitchen had been extended by taking out the wall of an old scullery. Modern units had been installed, but another part of its earlier look was maintained by a wide fireplace, where a large cooking pot would have once hung over an open fire.

Another room, originally the bedroom, had been converted by the previous owner into a small lounge, retaining the old brick surround fireplace and red tiled floor. Ben instinctively felt there was something odd about the room, but he couldn't place it.

On the first floor the extension provided three bedrooms. Ideal thought Ben for friends and family to stay on visits.

There wasn't much improvement he could make inside the main property, which led him to question, like his wife, why it was on sale well below market value. The outbuildings at the side could be greatly improved, but that wouldn't account entirely for the low price.

"The last owners were wealthy people. Bought the property and did it up after it had been derelict for some years," Justin explained, "then I believe they decided to move abroad. Wanted a quick sale."

To Ben it sounded like an estate agent story, but he was captured by the setting. All around beautiful green meadows with crisp fresh air. Even though late autumn was approaching, the sun blazing in a clear blue sky radiated welcoming warmth through his being.

Beside the farmhouse a wide stony track led to several disused storage outbuildings lining the route, the old walls crumbling and the roofs on them virtually caved in.

The thought returned to Ben they'd be ideal to renovate and offer as holiday lets. Even in retirement he and Eleanor could earn some money from the summer season. The appeal of potential grew in his mind, pushing further away the curiosity of why the farmstead was being sold so cheaply.

Justin smiled inwardly, sensing his client was keen on the property, and glad that Ben's obvious attraction to the setting had distracted him from any close questioning that might lead to the farmhouse's dark history. The sales deal was sealed.

Back home, Eleanor still had misgivings about the purchase, but her husband had made many successful decisions and deals in the past, so she was guided by his plan. And it would be good to share more leisure time together after spending so many years on business, which on reflection had stolen a large chunk of their lives.

A couple of months later the sale completed. Ben gathered his sleeping bag and building equipment which he'd used a number of years back when he worked away from home on projects. The couple had agreed Eleanor would remain looking after the business in the office, while he set off in their Transit van to do some preliminary work preparing the outbuildings for renovation. The first step in the new venture.

But despite this growing positive in life, Eleanor could not rid the sense of dread that kept haunting her. The troubled dreams had continued. She waved goodbye to her husband on the driveway. A terrible omen of it being the last time she would see him alive made her shiver, as if she'd been clasped by a cold embrace from the grave.

BEN felt tired after the long, three-hundred mile drive to the west Cornwall farmhouse. He'd brought along a few home convenience comforts and set about heating a ready meal shepherd's pie in the microwave he'd installed in the kitchen.

He placed a couple of canvas chairs and a trestle table in the living room to make it look a little more homely, then settled himself at the table to eat the pie accompanied with a can of beer. He finished the meal and rested back in the chair starting to feel sleepy, his head slowly sinking towards his chest.

He woke with a jerk.

For a second Ben thought he'd heard a voice. Someone calling. He got up and opened the living room door into the hall, looking around.

"Hello," he called, wondering if a neighbour had come to the property to greet him. There was no reply. He must have imagined the sound while nodding off into sleep after dinner.

The early winter sun hovered low in the sky as twilight approached. Just time for Ben to carry out a bit of reconnaissance on the farmhouse outbuildings he'd earmarked for preliminary alteration. He could demolish the remaining sections of collapsing roofs, but work by his construction crews would be needed for later restoration.

As Ben walked down the track behind the farmhouse, checking the condition of the decaying buildings, the atmosphere seemed strangely quiet. He went inside one of them. The slate roof had almost entirely collapsed, rubble scattered across the floor, leaving the building open to the sky.

Flapping wings made him look up. Two brown hawks settled on top of the stone sidewall, staring at him inquisitively. Their sharp beaks, highly efficient at ripping apart small animals and carrion, seemed poised to launch at him. Ben suddenly felt vulnerable to attack. After a few moments the birds flapped their wings and took off, soon disappearing into the fading light of the sky.

He was a man with nerves of steel. But their presence had sent a shiver through him. He put it down to the chill air. Silly to feel unsettled by hawks. They don't usually bother humans. Returning to the farmhouse, he resolved to start demolishing the remaining section of the outbuilding's roof first thing in the morning.

Ben made a cup of coffee in the kitchen then realised it was time to ring Eleanor. She wanted to know he'd arrived safely. He dialled, but the call wouldn't connect. He saw the phone wasn't receiving a signal. This was an out of the way place and likely that connections were unreliable. Ben hoped his wife wouldn't worry. Especially if she was trying to call him. She knew he'd be okay he reasoned.

To while away a few evening hours he played some stored video games on the tablet he'd brought along. That, and a few beers kept him entertained in his loneliness. Then he made his way upstairs to the bedroom where he looked forward to settling with Eleanor when the place was furnished and they'd moved in.

For now a sleeping bag on the floor would have to do. The spartan bedding reminded him of his earlier days as a young man, staying in portakabins and mobile homes while working on contracts around the country.

Although he'd arranged for the farmhouse to be reconnected with electricity, he kept a torch handy beside him. From past experience he knew some of the more remote places could suffer power cuts if the weather turned stormy.

He turned off the light, a single bulb hanging from the centre of the ceiling on a short cord, and climbed into the sleeping bag. There were no curtains to shade the silver glow from the moonlight shining through the window overlooking the side track of the farmhouse.

Ben thought of Eleanor and all the days they could spend together enjoying a country life. After working so hard they deserved the chance of a more leisurely pace.

He must have fallen asleep, because the sound of voices made him open his eyes with a start. Surely there couldn't be anyone else in the place? He sat up listening intently. The silence almost hummed. The moonglow seemed to cast a strange atmosphere of another world not quite within earthly grasp

After a few moments he dismissed the sense of something not being right, deciding he'd just heard voices in a dream, and settled down. Soon after, he awoke to the voices again. They were coming from downstairs. Maybe it was another dream, but he decided to check.

Ben got up and flicked on the light switch. It didn't work. The room remained in moonlight. A power failure already? He grabbed the torch just as the sound of voices now came from the side track below the window. He crossed to it and looked down to see the shadowy outbuildings in the moonglow, but no presence.

His heart began pumping quickly. He switched on the torch to search downstairs. Perhaps a property left unoccupied attracted tramps for a comfortable night's accommodation.

He opened the bedroom door and shone the torch beam along the landing, making his way to the stairs. At the top he directed it down the stairwell. It lit a well rounded, middle-aged woman standing at the bottom. She wore a dark grey dress with a white apron and linen mob cap. The clothing appeared to be from an age long past. She stared at him with a calculating smile, assessing him like a victim for a terrible fate. Ben almost dropped the torch in shock.

As he stared back, her image disappeared and the torchlight displayed just the empty flagstone hall floor where she'd stood. He remained still, his mind confused, attempting to take in what he'd seen. He didn't believe in ghosts...and yet?

OTHER BOOKS BY THE AUTHOR

All available on Amazon

THE LOST VILLAGE HAUNTING

Ghosts rise from an old village that long ago fell into the sea.

EMILY'S EVIL GHOST

Ghosts reveal murderous horror in a haunted country house.

DEADLY ISLAND RETREAT

Trapped on a remote island with ghosts and horrifying revelations. Also in Audible

DARK SECRETS COTTAGE

Shocking family secrets unearthed in a haunted cottage.

THE SOUL SCREAMS MURDER

A family faces terror in a haunted house.

THE BEATRICE CURSE

Burned at the stake, a witch returns to wreak revenge.

THE BEATRICE CURSE 2

Sequel to the Beatrice Curse

A GHOST TO WATCH OVER ME

A ghostly encounter exposes horrific revelations.

A FRACTURE IN DAYBREAK

A family saga of crime, love and dramatic reckoning.

VENGEANCE ALWAYS DELIVERS

When a stranger calls – revenge strikes in a gift of riches.

THE ANARCHY SCROLL

A perilous race to save the world in a dangerous lost land.

THE TWIST OF DEVILS

Four short stories of devilish manipulation.

MORTAL TRESPASSES

A mysterious phone call leads to a secret sect raising the dead.

For further information contact Geoffrey Sleight
email: geoffsleight@gmail.com

Amazon Author page:
https://www.amazon.com/author/geoffreysleight

Twitter:
@resteasily

Goodreads:
https://www.goodreads.com/geoffreysleight

Printed in Great Britain
by Amazon

19006380R00099